AMELIA FANG
and the
HALF-MOON HOLIDAY

LAURA ELLEN ANDERSON

EGMONT

CONTENTS

THE SUGARPLUM TREE

BUGGINGTONSHIRE

Miniopolis

LITTLE LAKE

SUGARPLUM ISLAND

THE EMPTY CAVES

THE SEA of SPARKLES

NG DOCKS

SPARKLE SPA

LEPRECHAUN LAGOON

Ghoulish Greetings!

AMELIA FANG

AND SQUASHY

LIKES:
Hanging out with friends
Pumpkin Paradise Park!

DISLIKES:
Mean creatures
Tidying up her bedroom

LIKES:
His special eyelid cream
New clothes

DISLIKES:
Running out of eyelid cream
Being hungry

TANGINE

AND PUMPY

FLORENCE

LIKES:
Boat races
Foraging for food

DISLIKES:
Tangine's eyelid cream obsession
Being called a 'Beast'

GRIMALDI

LIKES:
Being with his friends
His trusty scythe torch

DISLIKES:
What's in the Sea of Sparkles
Tragic stories

GRAHAM

LIKES:
Telling tragic stories
Sandwiches with extra filling

DISLIKES:
Ricky's map reading
Running out of teabags

RICKY

LIKES:
The Rainbow Ranger club
Summer Houses

DISLIKES:
Graham's tragic storytelling
Graham's driving

FRANKIE

LIKES:
His Nectar Carriage
His bug kingdom

DISLIKES:
Anything with butter
An unhappy bug

LIKES:
Being the best in class
Tormenting Amelia Fang

DISLIKES:
Amelia getting better grades
Being nice

KING JAMIE VIII

CHAPTER 1
SPARE KNICKERS

As the sun rose in the Kingdom of the Dark, the creatures of Nocturnia were all getting ready for bed; all apart from one little vampire and her pet pumpkin, Squashy.

'*Muuuum!*' Amelia Fang called up the spiral staircase of the Fang Mansion. 'Have you seen my pumpkin backpack? I need it for the Rainbow Rangers camping trip, and I have to be in Central Nocturnia Graveyard in ten minutes to meet everyone!'

A yellow door halfway down the corridor burst open and Countess Frivoleeta, a beautiful vampiress with VERY tall hair, appeared. She was wearing a long sparkly dressing gown with HUGE shoulder pads and her hair was wrapped up in a glittery towel.

'Darkling!' she oozed, scooping Amelia up in her arms. 'I can't believe you're going away for the *whole* half-moon holiday!' She kissed Amelia three times on each cheek, leaving behind shiny black lipstick marks. 'Now, did you remember your fang polish? How about your pale skin scrub? Oh, and some spare pairs of knickers just in case any get eaten by vultures or something . . .'

'Mum!' Amelia blushed. 'None of my things will get eaten by vultures. Plus, we're going to the Kingdom of the

Light. You don't really get any vultures over there. But I really do need to find my pumpkin backpack or I won't be able to pack a spare pair of *anything*.'

The countess pondered for a moment and then disappeared into her bedroom. A few seconds later, she emerged from another room further along the corridor. The doors of the Fang Mansion were rather unusual; they moved around whenever they pleased and Amelia was lucky if her bedroom was behind the same door for more than a few weeks at a time. Some doors disappeared, new ones appeared and you never knew quite where you were going to end up!

'You can use *this* bag if you like? It's one of my favourites!' said the countess, stroking a furry clutch bag which looked like a flattened mouse. Amelia was unsure she'd fit her hand inside it let alone a week's worth of camping essentials. As Amelia tried to figure out a way to let her mother down gently, her dad appeared from the bathroom with a crossword puzzle tucked under one arm.

'Ah! My favourite sausage sizzler!' said Count Drake the Third when he saw Amelia. 'You must be excited to escape organ practice for a whole week!' He winked mischievously.

Countess Frivoleeta glared at her husband. 'Drake my most dreadful flabbergaster, Amelia will be catching up with her organ practice after the half-moon holiday, won't you, darkling?'

Amelia sighed. 'Yeess, Mum.'

The Fang Mansion Grimfather clock chimed, causing Amelia to shriek.

'It's already 5am! *I'm going to be late!*' she said, running along the corridor. 'Where's my backpack?!'

Squashy bounced around in circles,

waggling his stalk and squeaking in shared panic.

'Do you mean *this* backpack, young Amelia?' came a familiar voice from the bottom of the stairs.

Wooo, the most respected ghost butler in the Kingdom of the Dark, floated up towards them holding a round orange bag.

'Oh, Wooo!' said Amelia, running over to him. 'You're the best!'

'I found it in the basement being cradled by a bogeyman. He'd adopted it as his pet.' Wooo turned to the count and countess. 'I'm afraid the bogeyman infestation is getting worse. We'll need to move them on quickly otherwise they'll start to take over the whole house. They'll wear *all* your clothes, Countess, and then rip them up. *For fun.*'

Countess Frivoleeta looked as though she might faint, and her left eyeball was spinning

around so quickly it was dangerously close to falling out.

'It's okay, my dearest little pus-fart. We'll sort it.' Count Drake nodded at Wooo and took a deep breath. 'I'll call the Bogey Busters tonight.'

With her pumpkin backpack filled to the brim, a few spare pairs of knickers (JUST IN CASE) and a very bouncy Squashy, Amelia kissed her mum and dad goodbye. She was so nervous, her tummy felt full of fluttering vampire moths. She'd never been away from home for this long before without her parents; not even when she ventured to Glitteropolis to find Tangine's mum.

Countess Frivoleeta straightened Amelia's Rainbow Rangers sash. 'I expect this will be

FULL of badges by the time you return.'
The countess smiled. 'You're going to have the *best* time.'

'I hope so!' said Amelia. 'I'll miss you and dad though.'

'Oh, you'll forget all about missing us when you're having fun with your friends, my little toe-stopper,' said Amelia's mum. 'You won't want to come home!'

'And don't go eating anything you shouldn't,' said Count Drake.

Amelia giggled. 'Don't worry, Dad. I won't. A Rainbow Ranger must always be prepared. Plus, our Ranger leaders, Ricky and Graham, will be looking after us the whole time.'

'Well, you take care, my little pimple-popper.' Her dad smiled and gave Amelia a squeeze. He opened the vine-covered door that revealed a misty Central Nocturnia Graveyard.

'Right then,' said Amelia.
'My very first camping trip!
This is going to be the best half-
moon holiday ever!'

And with a wide-eyed Squashy tucked under
one arm, she stepped into the gloomy haze.

Amelia felt the spongy ground of the graveyard beneath her feet and breathed in the crisp night air. Squashy pa-doinged around her ankles and bounced across to where a whole mishmash of excitable creatures were gathered; from zombies and yetis to ghosts, werewolves and serpents. At the front of the crowd were two large unicorns, each wearing a rainbow-coloured scarf tied around their necks and a peaked cap with a rainbow logo sewn on to the front.

'Galloping gaffer tape!' said one of the unicorns. 'You see that tree there, Ricky?'

The unicorn called Ricky looked towards

a blackened spiky tree. 'Yeah, I see it, Graham . . .'

'Well, don't you think it looks a bit like me?' said Graham.

'Nah. I was thinking it looked much more like me actually. Bit broader in the shoulders, good set of elbows . . .' Ricky paused, then added, 'and bigger hooves.'

'Well, it probably reminds both of you of, well, *both* of you,' said Amelia as she approached. 'It's the famous Petrified-Tree-That-Looks-Like-a-Unicorn.'

Ricky and Graham looked at each other then said at the same time, 'definitely looks more like me.'

Amelia giggled at the two unicorns. She had already met Ricky and Graham, back when they were unicorn guards in Glitteropolis. Since then, Ricky and Graham had quit their guard duties, moved to Nocturnia and started the Rainbow Rangers club.

'Good to see you this fine half-moon holiday, Amelia Fang.' Graham gave a dramatic bow as Amelia skipped backwards out of the way of his very sharp unicorn horn.

'The half-moon holiday is my favourite time of year. Although it *is* the first time I've spent it away from home,' said Amelia with a slightly nervous fang-filled smile.

'Be brave, little Creature of the Dark,' said Ricky, wagging a reassuring hoof in Amelia's direction. 'Rainbow Rangers look after each other so you will be fine. And besides, me and Graham have got big plans for this trip, you won't have hardly any time at all to feel homesick!'

'Oh, I sure hope so . . .' whispered a high-pitched voice from behind Amelia.

'Hi, Grimaldi!' Amelia hugged the little grim reaper, who had floated up beside her.

'I'm nervous too but I am *so* excited to go camping together. No school for a whole week!'

'*And* no scraping small dead creatures off the streets!' Grimaldi added, waving his scythe around. 'My grimpapa will have to take care of that while I'm away.' Grimaldi Reaperton was a tiny reaper who dealt with the deaths of small creatures around Nocturnia. And even though Death was his middle name, he was actually scared of almost everything.

Suddenly, a CRASH was heard as the ground burst open a few feet away from Amelia and Grimaldi. The little reaper shot a mile into the air and Squashy squeaked and bounced into Amelia's arms for comfort. A gravestone went hurtling through the air, followed by a very confused zombie's head.

'*My heeeeeeeeeeeeead*!' the head screeched, as it rolled away into the woods.

Where the grave once stood, a huge yeti, NOT to be confused with a beast, emerged.

'IT'S THE 'ARF MOON 'OLIDAY!' bellowed Florence Spudwick. 'NO SCHOOOOOOL!'

'Hi, Florence!' replied Grimaldi and Amelia in unison.

Florence had been practising her pit digging every night. A super-special yeti skill, Florence had now mastered the art of digging her way around the city, creating her very own nifty network of underground tunnels – the latest of which ended right where the gravestone had once stood.

Prince Tangine La Floofle the First was the last of the Rainbow Rangers to arrive, accompanied by the loud PA-DOOFS of his genetically modified pet pumpkin, Pumpy.

'Sorry I'm late,' Tangine said with a sigh. 'I HAD to apply my eyelid cream and let it dry before I could leave.'

Graham tapped his unicorn hooves impatiently and raised a sceptical eyebrow.

Prince Tangine was half-fairy, half-vampire and rather fond of his nightly skin care routine. He was also one of Amelia's best friends, along with Florence and Grimaldi.

'WHAT THE BATS ARE YOU PUTTING EYELID CREAM ON FOR?' said Florence.

'To prevent them from drooping,' said Tangine with an air of superiority. 'You'll be sorry when your eyelids get all droopy and I still look RAVISHING.'

Florence was just about to tell Tangine exactly what she

thought of his eyelids when Ricky the unicorn interrupted the excited chitter chatter of the group with an announcement.

'Good morning Rainbow Rangers! Now you're all here, I can finally tell you where we'll be camping for the half-moon holiday. We will be staying in a remote and quiet little place called Sugarplum Island. It's surrounded by the sea and is just a few miles east of the Kingdom of the Light.'

There was a buzz of anticipation amongst the young Rainbow Rangers.

'Prepare yourselves for some awesome activities and the chance to earn yourselves a BUNCH of Rainbow Ranger BADGES,' Ricky continued.

'Oooh! I LOVE badges!' squealed Amelia. She was determined to fill up her Rainbow Ranger sash with as many badges as she could by the end of the half-moon holiday.

Who didn't love a badge?!

'Whoever gets the most badges by the end of the week will be awarded the position of Rainbow Ranger Captain!' Graham added.

The Rainbow Rangers cheered and high-fived each other excitedly.

'That will be ME, of course,' said a loud voice. Amelia, Florence and Grimaldi sighed. Frankie Steinburg was a ghoul in the same class as Amelia at school and it was just typical that she would join the Rainbow Rangers too. She was very competitive and constantly trying to outdo everyone.

'Okay, Rangers!' Graham called over the commotion. 'Before we leave, you know what to do . . . '

Amelia and the rest of the Rainbow Rangers lined up. They straightened their sashes and saluted before earnestly reciting the Rainbow Ranger Promise:

'In the brightest day and the gloomiest night,
Whether I'm a creature of Dark or of Light.

I will be patient and grateful and kind,
And never leave a fellow Ranger behind.

I'll strive to keep learning. I'll trek and explore.
And promise to keep the Rainbow Ranger Law.'

'I think I'm gonna cry,' said Ricky, dabbing at his eyes with his rainbow scarf.

Graham was already sobbing. 'Okay, Rainbow Rangers,' he said through his sniffles. 'Let's get this half-moon holiday adventure started!'

CHAPTER 3
THE OTHER LEFT

Amelia gazed through the Rainbow Wagon window as they trundled through the Kingdom of the Light, into the Meadow of Loveliness and past the Wishing Well of Well Wishes. Graham was driving and Ricky was giving directions.

'LEFT!' shouted Ricky suddenly, making everyone jump. 'No, wait . . . THE OTHER LEFT. LIGHT. I mean, RIGHT. REFT?'

'Oh my days, *Ricky*!' said Graham as he narrowly missed a bewildered looking pixie-hen in an apron. 'You're RUBBISH at this. Next time, YOU drive, and I'll read the map.'

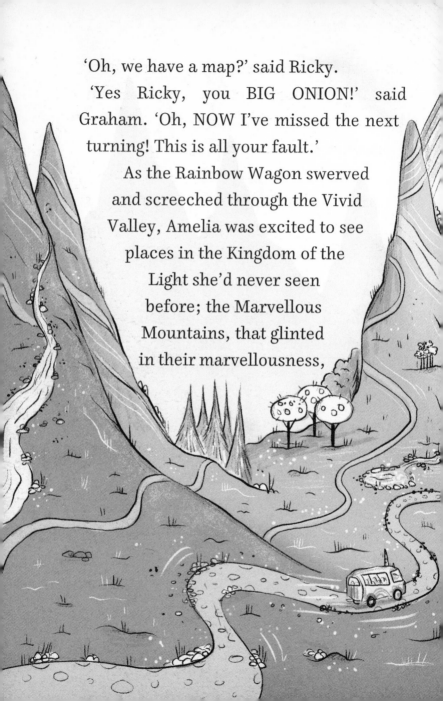

'Oh, we have a map?' said Ricky.

'Yes Ricky, you BIG ONION!' said Graham. 'Oh, NOW I've missed the next turning! This is all your fault.'

As the Rainbow Wagon swerved and screeched through the Vivid Valley, Amelia was excited to see places in the Kingdom of the Light she'd never seen before; the Marvellous Mountains, that glinted in their marvellousness,

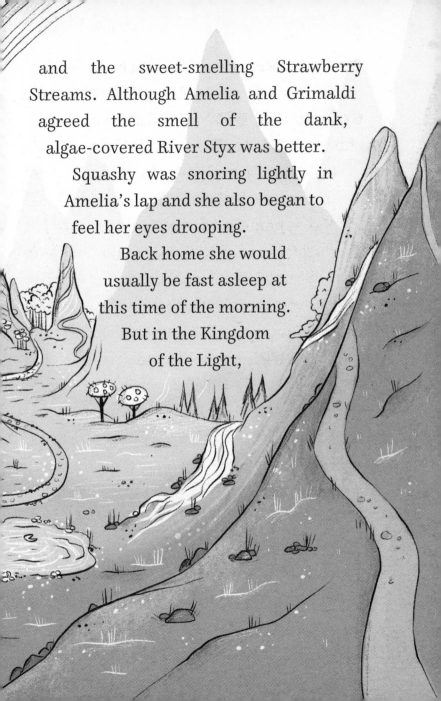

and the sweet-smelling Strawberry Streams. Although Amelia and Grimaldi agreed the smell of the dank, algae-covered River Styx was better.

Squashy was snoring lightly in Amelia's lap and she also began to feel her eyes drooping.

Back home she would usually be fast asleep at this time of the morning. But in the Kingdom of the Light, where the Rainbow Rangers were heading, things were the other way around. Amelia gave a big yawn.

After many winding roads and having scoffed too many sugary sweets, Grimaldi had managed to use every single sick bag available. He did not deal well with travelling for long periods of time. But finally, and much to everyone's relief, the Rainbow Wagon reached its destination; the Dazzling Docks. And boy were they dazzling – the sea sparkled fiercely, making the Rainbow Rangers squint and shield their eyes, as the shining waves lapped up on to the sandy beach.

'SO MUCH DAZZLE,' said Florence, shielding her eyes as she stepped out on to the soft sandy ground.

'Wow! I've never seen water like that before,' said Amelia, staring at the sea. The bright shimmering waves washed away the last of her sleepiness. 'It's so different to the Frogleg Falls or the Putrid Pond back home.'

'It's definitely more sparkly,' Grimaldi agreed, lifting a hand to cover his mouth. The brightness wasn't helping his travel sickness. 'I think after a week of all these bright colours, I'll be relieved to go back home to the grey murkiness of Nocturnia.'

The Dazzling Docks were packed full of little wooden boats all painted with different colours and patterns. Amelia liked the fact that each boat seemed to have its very own personality. Ricky and Graham had gathered the Rainbow Rangers on the pier where a huge sparkly polar bear with a wooden leg and an eye patch was waiting. Amelia thought he was a bit grizzly to be working in the Kingdom of the Light amongst the glittery fairies and cute puppy-dragons.

'Alright, you horrible lot, listen up!' said Ricky. 'The very nice Mr Shivery Tim Bear here, has kindly offered to lend us a bunch of his row boats to get across to Sugarplum Island.'

Mr Shivery Tim Bear grunted and nodded.

'And, GUESS WHAT?!' Graham added. 'This is your first chance to earn a badge.' He did an awkward wobbly twirl just to emphasise exactly how impressed everyone should be about this.

Grimaldi sniggered.

Mr Shivery Tim Bear stood next to Graham in silence. The polar bear didn't look very impressed.

'If you successfully cross the water without sinking, you could earn yourself your first badge! *But* . . .' Graham paused dramatically. 'You won't just be rowing across to the island . . .'

'Oof!' exclaimed Amelia, as Frankie pushed in front of her, eager to be first to hear how to win the new badge.

'You will be racing!' Ricky declared, taking over from Graham. 'The first Rainbow Ranger to reach the coast wins an *I GOT THERE FIRST* badge. So, in an orderly fashion, go and pick a vessel!'

Without hesitation, the Rainbow Rangers scrambled forwards, desperate to find a boat and win the race.

Florence pushed her way through the crowd and launched herself into a small polka dot boat. A huge wave of water rose in the air, soaking a shocked Ricky and Graham.

Amelia and Squashy made themselves comfortable in a black and white stripy boat, while Grimaldi found a swirly patterned one.

Tangine chose the most extravagantly decorated boat in the docks; adorned with four wrought iron posts and lavish frilly red curtains. It rather resembled a floating four-poster bed.

In the water next to Amelia was Frankie. Her narrow boat was covered in green spikes – it looked a bit like a floating cactus. 'Don't expect to beat me,' Frankie said with a glare, poising herself for the race.

Amelia rolled her eyes and braced her oars.

'Good luck Amelia,' whispered Grimaldi from the boat next to her. 'And make sure you don't let Frankie win!'

'Don't worry, I'll try my best!' Amelia said, smiling. She looked out towards Sugarplum Island as it glimmered on the horizon.

'Okay, Rangers!' Graham shouted across the docks to the eagerly waiting racing creatures. 'Before you set off, there is one thing to be aware of – there have been rumours of shadows beneath the waves of the Sea of Sparkles; wiggles in the tides and secrets in the sea spray . . .'

'Graham, you're doing your annoying *explaining-things-in-weird-ways-nobody-understands* thing,' said Ricky.

Graham sighed. 'Fine. There's weird stuff in the sea but no one knows what it is. *Okay*?'

The Rainbow Rangers muttered nervously amongst themselves and Grimaldi peered warily over the side of his swirly boat. Amelia leaned across and gave his hand a reassuring squeeze. 'Whatever it is, it can't be as bad as what lives in the Putrid Pond or beneath the Nocturnian graveyard, right?' Grimaldi giggled and nodded.

'You'll be fine!' Ricky reassured everyone with a big grin. 'Just stay in your boat and everything will be grand.' The Rainbow Rangers were silent.

Ricky cleared his throat. 'Alrighty then! Let's get this show started. Ready, steady . . . ROW!'

Nobody moved.

Apart from Florence.

'OH, COME ON WIMPITS! IT'S JUST A SILLY SEA STORY!' called their yeti classmate who was already ploughing through the waves using her own great paws instead of oars. 'THAT BADGE IS MINE!'

At the word 'badge' Frankie suddenly begun to row. '*I'm* totally getting the *I GOT THERE FIRST* badge!'

One by one, the Rainbow Rangers began to move away from the dock and then, when nothing odd seemed to happen in the water below, they each sped up until a fully-fledged race was on. Splashes and sploshes and shrieks of delight were heard as the Rainbow Rangers pulled themselves across the water.

'Come on Grimaldi, let's go!' Amelia called, setting off through the water as fast as she could row. But the little reaper was tucked away inside his boat, frozen to the spot.

'I . . . I'm worried about what's under there . . .' he peeped over the side of his boat.

Amelia saw her fellow Rainbow Rangers rowing away across the water and felt that extra badge slipping away, too. 'It's fine, Grimaldi!' she urged. 'Look, nothing is happening! Row next to me the whole way.' She smiled encouragingly. 'You can do it!'

Grimaldi hesitated, then pulled himself up

into a seated position. He began to slowly move away from the dock.

'That's it, you've got this!' said Amelia. 'Now, just move a *biiiiit* faster and then we can beat Frankie!'

Grimaldi began to pick up speed and soon the two friends were flying across the water to catch up with the rest of the Rangers.

Amelia rowed as fast as her little arms would go, with Grimaldi close behind. 'I knew all those years of rowing along the River Styx with Grimpapa would pay off!' he called out.

They giggled as they passed Tangine. Pumpy's end of the bed-boat was, rather tellingly, much further down in the water. They gradually overtook Rainbow Ranger after Rainbow Ranger. As Florence was whizzing through the water just ahead, Amelia had a brilliant idea.

'Hey Florence!' she yelled, slowing down a little, with Grimaldi following suit. 'If me, you and Grimaldi tie, then maybe we'll *all* get the bonus badge!'

'OOOH, GOOD FINKING AMELIA!' said Florence. The three friends rowed side by side and made for Sugarplum Island. They were SO close now! Then . . .

BOMP!

Something knocked the side of Amelia's boat sending her wobbling off course. She shrieked as the little stripy boat span out of control.

'Oops! Sorry! Didn't see you there,' Frankie said, smirking, and raced off in her spiky boat, overtaking Grimaldi and Florence who had slowed down to check their friend was okay.

'WANT ME TO GO SIT ON FRANKIE?' shouted Florence.

'You guys just keep going, and I'll meet you at the island!' Amelia replied, waving them forward. 'You still have a chance to beat Frankie! *Go, go, go!*'

She didn't mind being left behind just as long as Frankie *didn't* win.

Florence saluted, then she and Grimaldi raced on ahead to try and catch Frankie, as more and more Rainbow Rangers began to overtake Amelia's boat.

Suddenly, Amelia felt something damp on

her bottom. When she looked down, water was oozing into her boat.

'Oh, no,' Amelia gasped. One of the spikes on Frankie's boat had made a big hole in the side of Amelia's little stripy one. Squashy bounced into the growing puddle of water and tried to lick it up.

'It's okay, Squashy,' said Amelia, picking the pumpkin up and hugging him to her chest. 'I'm going to shout for help, then Ricky and Graham can come and rescue us.'

But just as Amelia was about to flag down the two unicorns, she felt a strong wind blowing back the hair from her face.

Her boat was moving.

CHAPTER 4
THE ISLAND IS YOUR PLATE

'How is this happening?' Amelia murmured, hugging Squashy tighter.

The little boat was heading straight for the shore of Sugarplum Island, overtaking all of her fellow Rainbow Rangers, and Amelia wasn't doing a thing!

Amelia peered warily over the side of the boat, feeling slightly nervous about what she might see. Ricky and Graham had warned them about odd things lurking beneath the water – perhaps they *were* right!

To Amelia's surprise, she couldn't see anything but her reflection and the bubbles created from the speed at which the boat was moving. But then Amelia thought she could *hear* something, a faint humming sound. She looked around, but everyone was too far behind her now for it to be any of her fellow Rainbow Rangers.

'Do you hear that, Squashy?' asked Amelia. She thought that she was even beginning to make out a tune. Squashy certainly seemed to be waggling his stalk from side to side in time with something . . .

But, before she knew what was happening, the boat ploughed itself up on to the sandy shore and Amelia could hear the tune no more. Amelia looked back at the water breathlessly, feeling utterly confused about what had just happened.

One by one the other Rainbow Rangers began to pull up on to the shore next to her including a red-faced Frankie Steinburg. 'You CHEATED!' she snapped, storming up to

Amelia's boat.

'Trust me, I really, *really* didn't,' said Amelia, still feeling confused. 'I didn't do anything!'

'You're LYING!' said Frankie, whose neck-bolt was spinning in anger.

'OH, SHOVE OFF,' said Florence, stomping over and pushing Frankie out of the way. 'WELL DONE, AMELIA! YOU'RE A ROWING CHAMPION!'

'You won the bonus *I GOT THERE FIRST* badge!' Grimaldi cheered as he arrived in his little boat.

Amelia shook her head. 'I . . . I . . . I didn't do anything!'

'DON'T BE SO MODEST!' Florence scooped Amelia up into a big hug. 'YOU WON FAIR 'N' SQUARE.'

The Rainbow Rangers gathered around Ricky and Graham as the two unicorns presented Amelia with her bonus *I GOT THERE FIRST* badge.

Frankie stood glaring at her, both arms folded across her chest.

'Welcome to Sugarplum Island!' said Ricky. 'We've got LOTS of exciting activities ahead of us this week. Graham has given each of you a special *Rainbow Ranger Guidebook*, which has a map of the island and tells you exactly what you need to do to earn each badge.

You have the whole half-moon holiday week to complete as many as you can.'

Tangine was flicking through his guidebook, when he suddenly stopped and put his hand up shakily. 'Um, excuse me, but this badge here says *FOOD FORAGING* badge?' He gulped. 'As in searching for your food? As in . . . you *won't* be serving us a three-course meal every night?'

'EXACTLY!' Ricky and Graham both looked very enthusiastic.

FOOD FORAGING
BADGE

HOW TO EARN YOUR BADGE:

FIND ENOUGH EDIBLE SOURCES OF FOOD FROM YOUR NATURAL SURROUNDINGS TO SUSTAIN YOU FOR ONE WEEK.

'You'll be learning to find your own food and prepare your own meals!' said Ricky. 'That's how you'll earn your *FOOD FORAGING* badge. Sugarplum Island is teaming with thousands of Bobbin-Berries, Frillyflowers and Dung-Pods of all shapes and sizes!'

'OOO, DUNG-PODS!' said Florence licking her lips. 'GONNA FIND ME A 'OLE BATCH O' THOSE!'

'We'll be eating off plates though, right?' said Tangine, looking a little wobbly. 'China plates? With swirly patterns?'

Graham looked down at Tangine and lowered his little glasses. 'Oh dear, *dear* Tangine . . . The island *is* your plate.'

Tangine held Amelia's shoulder for support. He took a deep breath. 'Everything will be fine. At *least* I have my eyelid cream with me.'

The Rainbow Rangers spent most of the afternoon setting up their tents and gathering kindling for a campfire.

As the sun began to set, everyone gathered around the fire to sing songs and toast Midnight Marshmallows.

Amelia kept admiring her *I GOT THERE FIRST* badge on her sash; but she couldn't help thinking she hadn't really earned it. Something else had helped her to win the boat race, but she had no idea what it was.

Tangine sat on a log studying the Sugarplum Island map. 'So, do any creatures live on this island?' he asked. 'And, more to the point, do any of them own a restaurant where I can get a nice cooked meal?'

'Ah . . . nobody has lived on this island for years,' said Graham. 'Only bizarre bugs and teeny-weeny creatures.' He shuffled his log closer to the fire. 'Years ago, many Creatures of the Light lived on the island. But gradually everyone left and no one really knows why . . .'

'They probably moved on before they got BORED to death . . .' said Tangine, yawning. 'Or starved from lack of quality waiter service.'

'I like the idea of foraging for food that's REALLY nearby,' a werewolf named Stink said, glaring at Tangine pointedly and licking his lips. 'But for now, why don't we tell tragic stories around the campfire?'

'Oooh, I have a story!' said Graham. 'Who wants to hear my story?'

The young Rainbow Rangers nodded and quiet descended over the group.

Graham cleared his throat and began. 'Once upon a time –'

'That's not how you should start a campfire story,' interrupted Ricky.

'Oi! You just RUINED my moment,' Graham huffed.

'Don't you know how a good campfire story works? You need to make it extra mysterious! Get the listener's attention straight away,' said Ricky, waving his hooves around dramatically. 'It sounds like you're about to tell us a *love* story or something.'

'No, it does not!' said Graham defensively. 'I'll have you know it's a TRAGIC story . . .'

'Bu–'

'ONCE upon a tiiiiime!' Graham sang so

loudly that Ricky's protests were completely drowned out. 'There was a unicorn named Graham who realised he'd run out of TEABAGS.'

The Rainbow Rangers looked confused.

'Wait. *This* is your tragic story?' said Stink, scratching his hairy ears with a hind leg in disappointment.

'How else would you describe running out of teabags?!' said Graham. 'Imagine setting yourself up with your favourite mug and a plate of biscuits, and then finding you can't make a cup of TEA!'

There was a long silence. One Rainbow Ranger had fallen asleep sitting up.

'*I* want to know what happens next!' said Amelia supportively. She felt bad for poor Graham.

Florence shot her a doubtful look.

Graham's eyes lit up. He sat up proudly and got ready to tell the rest of his story. But the Rainbow Rangers never got to find out what happened next. Because right at that moment, Gregory the goblin, who was sitting next to Frankie, sneezed loudly – and messily.

A HUGE globule of goblin snot flew into Frankie's face.

Frankie screamed and Amelia and the other Rainbow Rangers looked on in horror as Bobbin the bat flew RIGHT through Sylvia the ghost's tummy in fright.

Sylvia was outraged (you should NEVER pass through a ghost!).

And somehow, amidst the chaos, Kevin the cyclops set fire to his bottom.

CHAPTER 5

BEARDED BUGS

'Well, I guess that's story time over,' said Grimaldi. Amelia picked up a bewildered Squashy, to keep him safe from the stampeding Rainbow Rangers.

Graham galloped past, taking Kevin and his burnt bottom to the moonlit water.

'Well, I can't say I'm all that bothered about teabags or boring Sugarplum Island,' moaned Tangine. 'I'm HUNGRY. I can't possibly wait for Kevin's rear end to be extinguished before eating. I'm going to go get some of the Royal Snacks that Mum packed for me.'

Tangine opened his tent to reveal a very content Pumpy munching through a tub of Revolting Rhubarb Bites. Every other tub that once contained a Royal Snack was now empty.

'HEY! *Naughty pumpkin*! You've eaten ALL of my snacks!' Tangine snatched the tub away. He looked as if he may explode with anger. 'You're out of control, Pumpy!'

Squashy waggled his stalk in amusement from his safe spot in Amelia's arms.

'WE COULD GO FORAGE FER FOOD,' said Florence picking up a leaf and crunching it between her spiky teeth. 'IT'S YUMMY! TASTES A BIT LIKE MOULDY SPLEEN,' she added picking bits of leaf from the fur around her mouth.

Tangine huffed and walked further into the trees. 'Come on Pumpy,' he said sticking his nose in the air. 'Let's find a nice cheese and nostril baguette with extra toenail shavings.'

'Tangine, I don't think we're allowed to wander off,' said Grimaldi anxiously. 'Plus, Ricky and Graham said that nobody lives here anymore, so there won't be anywhere to buy food.'

'I don't believe that. Ricky and Graham are just *saying* there's no one around so that we hunt for food on the GROUND. Well, I'm not doing that,' declared Tangine. 'There has to be a shop or a restaurant around here SOMEWHERE.'

Amelia sighed and looked over towards the campfire. Stink the werewolf was howling at the half moon, and Sylvia the ghost was flying in circles wailing. Amelia's tummy rumbled and she had to admit Tangine had a point. Now it was night-time, she would usually be having her breakfast. 'Let's at least let Ricky and Graham know that we're going for a walk,' she said.

'Um, Ricky!' Amelia called over the chaos. But the two Rainbow Ranger leaders were busy trying to calm everyone down.

'Come on. Nobody is going to notice if we're gone for a bit,' said Tangine. 'My hunger is far more important than anything else. When I get too hungry, I shed unnatural amounts of glitter!'

'EWW!' said Florence as Tangine marched out of sight.

'We can't let him wander off alone,' sighed Amelia. 'Remember, *'Never leave a fellow Ranger behind'*! We'll just have to make sure we return before Ricky and Graham notice we're gone.'

'Yeah, I don't want to get into trouble before the half-moon holiday has even started!' said Grimaldi, pulling at his hood nervously.

Amelia breathed in the warm night air as the friends trundled through a woodland made up of tall narrow trunks and an abundance of giant and exotic flowering plant life that they'd never seen in the Kingdom of the Dark. Everything was so pleasingly dead and rotten back home.

Florence assessed the forest floor for potential pit digging, and Grimaldi floated around the trees, round and round the trunks, over and under the branches. His scythe had an inbuilt torch, which was very handy for guiding the friends through the darkness.

Tangine had his *Rainbow Ranger Guidebook* in his hand and was studying the map on the inside page. 'I think we should head THIS way,' he said, pointing ahead. 'There's bound to be a nice place to eat at the top of the mountain.'

'I AIN'T CLIMBING NO MOUNTAIN,' said Florence.

'Fine,' said Tangine, turning around, ready to stomp off. 'I'll see you later then.'

'YOU'RE BEING A STUBBORN LUMP!' huffed Florence after him.

Suddenly, an orderly procession of bearded bugs flew past Florence's head.

'ARGH!' she bellowed. 'I FINK ONE WENT IN MY EAR!' The little bugs scattered as she flailed her wonderfully large and hairy arms around.

Pumpy, quickly seizing the opportunity, PA-DOOFED up into the air and gobbled up one of the bugs.

'NO, PUMPY!' Tangine yelled. 'STOP EATING ALL THE TIME!'

The bugs squealed and their little eyes turned bright green with indignation. They headed straight for Tangine.

'Uh oh . . .' Tangine ran as fast as he could into the mountainous woods with the bugs close behind him. Seeing his trail of potential food flying away, Pumpy followed as fast as his heavy load could carry him.

'*Tangiiiiine!*' Amelia called out. 'Quick! We'd better run after him or we'll lose him!'

Amelia, Grimaldi, Florence and Squashy made their way through the woods as fast as they could. They jumped over mini streams and shimmery flowers that occasionally erupted with little POOFS of glitter.

'WHERE DID 'E GO?!' said Florence, wheezing.

Amelia was beginning to panic. Tangine was nowhere to be seen and her legs were starting to ache as they ran up the impossibly tall and dark mountain. 'TAAAANGIIIIINE?!' she called out. '*Where are you*?!'

Higher and higher, Amelia and her friends climbed and ran and stumbled and stepped, until suddenly the most unexpected sight stopped them in their tracks . . .

CHAPTER 6
THAT GHOST PIE SANG TO THE PIGEON AT DAWN

'Wow!' Amelia gasped.

A ledge was carved out of the mountainside and on it an incredible garden stretched before them. The whole scene was lit up by a beautiful tree.

'I've never seen a glowing tree before!' said Grimaldi.

Florence stomped over to the tree through the long grass. 'IT'S FULL OF ROUND FINGS.

SOME KIND OF FRUIT OR SUMMIN'. THAT'S WHAT'S GLOWING.'

The tree was a sight to behold, with curly branches weaving their way around each other. From each branch dangled a plump yellow fruit, a bit like a Nocturnian Pungent Plum, just less maggoty and stinky. They glowed a bright yellow-gold.

Pumpy was happily munching on some of the glowing plums that had dropped to the ground. Tangine was slumped on the grass next to him catching his breath.

'The bugs flew away when we got here!' Tangine said, panting. 'And look what I found! A tree with EDIBLE fruit.' He reached up to a low hanging branch and picked one of the golden plums. 'Mmmmmmm . . . Try one!' He said through a mouthful.

Florence picked one of the glowing yellow plums from a curly branch and took a cautious bite.

'GOBBLING GRIPES!' said Florence, taking another bite. 'YOU'RE RIGHT. IT'S JUST LIKE BITING INTO A WONDERFULLY CONSTRUCTED YETI PIT!'

'That's not a taste,' said Tangine.

'WELL, I CAN'T FINK WHAT IT TASTES LIKE . . . JUST SUMMIN' REALLY, REALLY GOOD!' said Florence, picking another five plums and stuffing them into her mouth all at once.

'I feel like we should go back to camp now,' Grimaldi said a little hesitantly. 'We weren't meant to wander off this far . . .'

'Grimaldi's right,' said Amelia. She stroked her Rainbow Rangers sash thoughtfully. 'But I guess this *could* count as foraging for food . . .'

Her mind made up, Amelia reached

purposefully for a plum. It was velvety and light and its gentle glow illuminated her pale skin. Amelia took a small bite and felt her mouth begin to water. The flavour was full and sweet and almost magical . . . like nothing she'd ever tasted before. She took another bite, and another.

All of a sudden, Amelia had forgotten about the urgency to get back to camp, and she was overwhelmed by the feeling of being very, *very* hungry.

'*Thish ish delishush*!' Amelia said through a mouthful. She picked another plum and held it out to Grimaldi. 'Come on, Grimaldi. It's not going to bite!' She giggled. 'We can record it in our Rainbow diaries to go towards our *FOOD FORAGING* badge!'

Grimaldi took it and cautiously bit into it. His eye sockets widened, and he smiled. 'Wow! This *is* good. No wonder it's glowing!'

Florence stared at the night sky, looking content. 'S'NICE 'ERE,' she said.

'It is,' Amelia yawned. She was beginning to feel unusually sleepy. 'We should probably head back before we get too comfortable.' The world around Amelia grew hazy and peaceful. She was aware that she needed to walk back to camp, but instead she found herself lying down in the grass. She turned over and reached down to snuggle up with

Squashy, who had already begun lightly snoring at her feet.

'ANYONE ELSE REALLY WANT A NAP RIGHT NOW?' came Florence's voice. Then she gave an almighty yawn and slumped to the floor next to a snoring Tangine.

What's happening? Amelia thought sleepily.

She felt Grimaldi curling up beside her. 'We should get back,' he whispered. 'Just five more minutes . . .'

'THAT GHOST PIE SANG TO THE PIGEON AT DAWN, DIDN'T IT?' said Florence. 'WE SHOULD SEND 'IM A LETTER . . .'

'Yeah,' said Amelia without thinking. 'Wait . . . *what*?' she thought as she slowly realised how little sense Florence was making. Amelia's eyelids felt so heavy.

Maybe I should close them just for a second, she thought. They were still getting used to the time difference in the Kingdom of the Light, after all.

Amelia closed her eyes and fell asleep to the sounds of Tangine snoring, Florence's jumbled sleep conversations and shuffling footsteps in the distance.

When Amelia woke, the full-moon was bright.
She sat up and rubbed her eyes in confusion.
The moon was meant to be a half-moon – it
was the half-moon holiday after all . . . But as
Amelia came to she noticed even more moons.

More moons?

What?

Amelia realised that what she was staring at weren't actually full moons at all. They were the glowing plums on the tree. Except they were much MUCH bigger than before.

Florence sleep-burped and woke herself up. 'YEESH,' she said. 'THEY'VE GROWN BIG.'

Grimaldi yawned and rose slowly, followed by a rather agitated Tangine.

'Where's my eyelid cream?' the prince mumbled. 'I NEED my eyelid cream *right now*! Pumpy, did you eat it?'

Pumpy responded with one PA-DOOF and rolled over on to a sleepy Squashy.

Amelia looked around to see that the grass they'd been lying on had grown too. But not by a little bit – it was now three times as tall as Florence. And the *Rainbow Ranger Guidebooks* that they'd been able to hold in one hand, were now the size of tents.

'Hold on . . .' said Amelia as the world around her began to make sense. She looked up and saw leaves as big as boats and flowers as big as houses.

'I don't think the plums are bigger,' she said, feeling her stomach twist. 'I think WE are much, *much* smaller . . .'

CHAPTER 7
SOPHISTICATED LADYBIRD WITH A BRIEFCASE

'WE'VE BEEN SHRINKED!' Florence shrieked. 'AAAAAAARGH!' She began panic-digging a tiny pit.

Grimaldi held shakily on to a blade of grass whilst Tangine stood with his hands on his hips, huffing and puffing. 'Well this just isn't good enough!'

'Okay, calm down everyone,' said Amelia, taking a few deep breaths. 'It's all going to be fine.' But Amelia had no idea whether it was going to be okay or not. She didn't know what else to say. Before she fell asleep, she was normal size, and had been very proud of the fact she'd grown a whole inch since last year.

But now, well *now* she was the size of a –

'SOPHISTICATED LADYBIRD WITH A BRIEFCASE!' Florence yelled from her tiny pit. And she was indeed pointing at a sophisticated looking ladybird wearing a tie and carrying a large briefcase.

'*I say*!' said the ladybird in a deeper voice than Amelia had expected. 'Did nobody tell you it's RUDE to point at a ladybird. Especially a sophisticated one.' Then he walked off in a huff through the tall grass.

'Wait!' Amelia called after the ladybird. 'Hello?! We need help! We're . . .Well, we're the wrong size!'

The ladybird reappeared with a frown. 'What *are* you going on about?'

Amelia felt a little embarrassed. 'Um, you

see, sir, we're not usually this small. We're usually much MUCH bigger.'

'YEH, LIKE WE COULD TREAD ON YOU KINDA SIZE,' said Florence, her head poking out from her pit. The ladybird frowned harder.

'Don't listen to her,' said Tangine, stepped forward. 'Florence doesn't know the meaning of sophistication like you and I.'

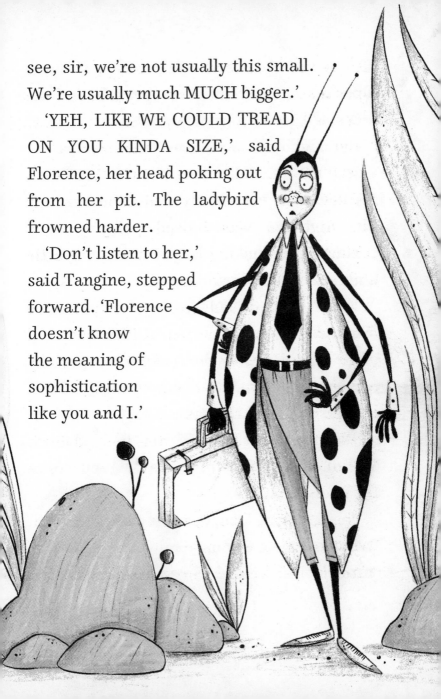

He leaned forward and whispered. 'I don't suppose you have any spare eyelid cream in that briefcase of yours, do you?'

The ladybird raised his thick eyebrows. 'And what are *you*? Some kind of moth?'

Tangine gasped and stroked one of his wings protectively. 'How *dare* you!'

'Guys!' said Amelia urgently. '*The pumpkins*! Where are Squashy and Pumpy?'

'I haven't seen them yet,' said a still shaky Grimaldi.

The ladybird with the briefcase rolled his eyes and turned away. 'You are very, VERY strange bugs and you are making me late for my dinner. So, goodbye!' and with that he walked away, grumbling a few grumpy words under his breath.

'RUDE!' said Florence.

'Come on, Tangine. We have to find our pumpkins!' said Amelia, and swiftly ran off in

80

no particular direction.

Amelia and Tangine weaved in and out of huge blades of grass, dodging pebbles the size of armchairs and Florence-sized loose plums.

'*SQUASHYYYY*! *PUMPYYYY*! WHERE ARE YOUUUU?!' Amelia yelled. 'They could be ANYWHERE,' she said to Tangine desperately.

Suddenly, Amelia heard a SNAP.

'What was that?' said Tangine.

Amelia looked around her, but there was nothing there. 'It sounded like it came from above . . .' and then the realisation hit her. 'Oh, no,' she cried.

It all happened so fast.

Amelia looked up to see a huge plum plummeting downwards straight towards her and Tangine; getting bigger and bigger by the second. She didn't have time to think before she was sent flying backwards. Something solid hit her smack bang in the middle of her stomach, causing the air to leave her lungs as she hit the ground.

There was an almighty THUD as the huge yellow plum crashed to the ground in the exact spot where Amelia and Tangine had been standing.

Amelia lay there in shock for a few seconds as she caught her breath, then saw the familiar black eyes and cheery smile of her pet pumpkin peering down at her.

'SQUASHY!' she said, almost crying. Amelia scooped him up into a tight hug, never wanting to let go.

Tangine was still flat on his back, with a very proud looking Pumpy sitting on his chest.

'Pumpy!' He wheezed. 'I. Can't. Breathe.'

Luckily, Pumpy spotted a mushroom nearby. He PA-DOOFED off Tangine's chest straight over to where it grew and began nibbling at its giant stalk.

Tangine sighed. 'I will never be as good as food to that pumpkin,' he said.

'AMELIA? GRIMALDI?' came Florence's voice. 'WHERE ARE YOU?'

'Over heeeere!' Amelia called back.

Eventually Florence appeared through the grass followed by Grimaldi, who was flinching at every noise and plant he brushed past.

'AH, YOU FOUND 'EM!' said Florence, giving Squashy a tickle on the stalk.

'Yeah, they actually saved us from a falling fruit,' said Amelia. 'We're going to have to be extra careful while we're so small.'

'But we won't be staying this size forever – *will we*?' squeaked Grimaldi.

'Of course not,' said Amelia. But she couldn't think exactly how they were going to get big again. She thought hard. 'We were eating the fruit just before this all happened,' she said suddenly. 'Maybe it's something to do with that?'

'How on earth can eating fruit make you shrink? Eating it is meant to make you GROW,' said Tangine. 'That's what Mum and Dad tell me anyway.'

The mention of the words 'Mum and Dad' made Amelia's tummy feel all tight.

She missed her parents very much already and the thought of not being able to get back to them made it a hundred times worse.

'What do we do now?' said Grimaldi.

'Well,' said Amelia. 'Ricky and Graham are the grown-ups in charge so we need to get back to camp and tell them what's happened. I'm sure they'll know what to do . . .' she added a little unsurely.

'BUT IT'LL TAKE US FOREVER TO GET BACK TO CAMP,' said Florence. 'EVERY FOOTSTEP IS LIKE A MILE TO US NOW!'

A huge drop of water landed on Florence, soaking her fur from head to toe.

SPLOSH!

'EURGH!' she cried. 'WOT WAS THAT?!'

SPLOSH! SPLOSH! SPLOSH!

'I think it might be –' Amelia gasped as another *SPLOSH* of water hit her, almost knocking her over with the force of it. *'Raaaaaaain!'*

CHAPTER 8

NO SIGN,
NO HOPE

Amelia picked Squashy up and held him tight. 'The ground is going to turn into an ocean any minute!'

'Puddles are NOT as fun when you're this small!' shrieked Tangine, who was trying desperately to pick Pumpy up.

SPLOSH! SPLOSH! SPLOSH! SPLOSH! SPLOSH! SPLOSH!

The rain was getting heavier.

'Over here!' Grimaldi shouted from somewhere nearby. Amelia looked over and saw the little grim reaper floating towards them on a huge leaf.

Holding on to the pumpkins, Amelia, Tangine and Florence clambered on, trying their very hardest not to fall in.

'We've got to find shelter!' said Amelia, trying to protect Squashy from the rain with her stripy skirt.

'I GOT THIS!' said Florence leaning forward. She put both of her strong arms into the water and began paddling hard. The leaf boat glided speedily along the water and through the garden.

The light coming from the glowing tree began to fade as they rowed farther away from it, and, apart from the torch on Grimaldi's scythe, the friends were soon in complete darkness.

But then, when it seemed like they couldn't get any wetter, it stopped. Amelia could still hear the SPLOSHing of the rain behind them, so where were they? She squinted as her eyes started to get used to the lack of light. 'Is everyone okay?'

'I'm not even thinking about the state of my hair from all that rain, but yes,' said Tangine, patting his glittery head.

'I'M ALWIGHT . . .' Florence replied. 'I FINK ONE OF THE PUMPKIN'S WEED ON ME THOUGH . . . I KNOW IT'S NOT RAIN CUZ IT'S WARM.'

Squashy blushed and wiggled his stalk apologetically.

Amelia began to realise that she was able to see the outline of things around her. 'Guys, I think we're in a cave!'

The friends fell silent as they took in the scene around them. The cave floor was full of beautiful paintings of the island propped up against the walls and lots of giant jars of yellow jam.

But that wasn't even the weirdest part.

All over the cave walls, the days of the week
had been scratched into the stone. And next
to each day were the words: NO SIGN.

MONDAY – NO SIGN
TUESDAY – NO SIGN
WEDNESDAY – NO SIGN
THURSDAY – NO SIGN
FRIDAY – NO SIGN
SATURDAY – NO SIGN
SUNDAY – NO SIGN
MONDAY – NO SIGN
TUESDAY – NO SIGN
WEDNESDAY – NO SIGN

MONDAY – NO SIGN
TUESDAY – NO SIGN
WEDNESDAY – NO SIGN
THURSDAY – NO SIGN
FRIDAY – NO SIGN
SATURDAY – NO SIGN
SUNDAY – NO SIGN
MONDAY – NO SIGN

And then it started all over again. 'I wonder what it means?' Amelia muttered, stepping out of the leaf boat.

'How odd,' said Grimaldi staring at the scribbled walls with big wide empty eyes.

'How TASTY!' said Tangine from somewhere else within the cave, followed by gobbling sounds.

Amelia looked up and saw Tangine leaning into one of the giant jam jars. He was scooping out handfuls of the yellow gloop and wolfing it down. *Come taste this*!' he said through a mouthful.

'Tangine, I don't think you should do that . . .'

But Tangine wasn't listening. He leaned further into the jar, eager to get more of the

yellow jam. However this time, it was too far – and he fell right in.

'*Tangine!*' Amelia gasped. She clambered up the jar as fast as she could and stretched an arm into it. 'Grab my hand!' she said as Tangine flailed around in the sugary gloop.

Florence and Grimaldi came to help, holding Amelia by the waist so that she could lean her whole body in to reach Tangine. He was beginning to sink.

Pumpy bounced into the jar to try to save his owner, but his weight meant that he quickly sank to the bottom.

'PUMPY!' Tangine yelled, spraying a mouthful of jam.

There was a sudden BOMP, causing the jar to wobble. Florence and Grimaldi lost their footing and went tumbling with Amelia straight into the jar with Tangine and Pumpy. Squashy pa-doinged around the outside of the jar in a panic.

'*Don't bounce in*!' Amelia yelled from inside the jar, as Squashy poised himself to jump in. But her voice was muffled, and the little pumpkin was in a panic, desperate to get to her; with one big pa-doing he bounced into the jar.

The jam jar went tumbling to the ground, landing with an almighty CRASH!

The friends went rolling in every direction across the ground.

'Oh, bothersome beetroot!' came a croaky voice from above. Amelia and her friends froze.

'A perfectly good jar of jam ruined!' said the voice. There was a shuffling sound and then a SWEEP, SWEEP, SWEEP and some humming.

'I know that tune,' murmured Amelia. 'But where from . . .?' But before she had a chance to think about it, there was one big almighty *SWEEEEEEEP* and the gang found themselves – together with the broken remains of the jam jar, bits of cobweb, strands of coarse hair and a pile of toenail clippings – launched out of the cave, through the night air and into a patch of daisies.

CHAPTER 9
A CORN THAT BUMBLES

Outside the rain had stopped, but the ground was still very wet and the puddles were the size of pools. Amelia squelched through the grass to check that Squashy was okay. He waggled a jam-covered stalk at her reassuringly.

'I think Pumpy is still in the cave!' said Tangine in a panic.

'We'll find him, don't worry,' said Amelia, although she didn't like the thought of going back in the cave to meet whoever or whatever had thrown them out.

The croaky voice suddenly rumbled out of

the cave again. 'Out! Out! Pesky bugs!' and something went hurtling through the air landing with a THUD in the daisy patch next to them.

'PUMPY!' cried Tangine happily.

'What the bats just happened?' said Grimaldi shaking the last of the dust from his cloak hood. 'Who *was* that?'

Amelia's head felt fuzzy. 'I don't know,' she said. 'But I do know that whoever it was didn't want us there. We need to get back to the campsite as fast as we can, so Ricky and Graham can help us.'

'What if we're stuck this size forever?' said Grimaldi nervously.

Amelia didn't want to even think about that prospect.

'Don't be silly, Grimaldi,' she said slightly more sternly than she'd meant. 'I'm sorry. I didn't mean to snap.'

Florence put a big hairy arm around Amelia's shoulders. 'COME ON FANG. S'NOT LIKE YOU TO BE DOOM AND GLOOM. THAT'S GRIMALDI'S JOB!'

'Hey!' protested Grimaldi. Then he grinned. 'It's true though.'

Amelia smiled. She could always count on her friends to cheer her up when she was feeling sad. She hugged Squashy tightly and he nuzzled into her chest, when suddenly there was a low buzzzzzzzzzzzzzzzzzzz. It quickly began to get louder. Amelia looked down at her friends in confusion.

'S'NOT ME,' said Florence with a shrug.

There was a rustling sound from amongst the daisies. The buzzing stopped.

Amelia thought her cold vampire heart was going to beat right through her chest. *Whatever next*?! They hadn't even got far enough away from whatever was in the cave yet.

Grimaldi grabbed Amelia's arm and Tangine hid himself behind Pumpy.

Florence stepped forward so that she was in front of Amelia, Grimaldi and Tangine, and poised herself, shaking down her fur in what she hoped was an intimidating manner.

The stems parted and out flew a shocked looking bumblebee.

'Oh, do pardon me!' said the bee, adjusting a pair of little glasses. He was also wearing a crown, a cape and carrying a large staff with a glowing ball at the top. But that wasn't all. He had one long shiny and very pointy horn on his head. He held the staff out to get a better look at Florence. 'Dancing dandelions. You're not a be–'

'THAT'S RIGHT,' Florence bellowed. 'I AM NOT A BEAST! I'M A RARE BREED OF YETI!'

Florence did not appreciate being mistaken

for a beast. It happened sometimes, but she was sure to let somebody know if they made that mistake.

The horned-bumblebee took a step backwards. 'Oh, I do very much see that. What I was going to say was, you're not a *bee* . . . or any kind of bug for that matter. Yet, you're the *same size* as one.'

Florence narrowed her eyes. 'YEAH . . . YER RIGHT.'

'Please allow me to introduce myself. I am King Jamie the Eighth of Buggingtonshire,' the bumblebee declared confidently. 'And *I* am a *bumblicorn*.'

A bumblicorn?' said Amelia, peering out from behind Florence.

'Oh, hello!' The king laughed as, one-by-one, the others followed Amelia's lead. 'Yes, the bumbliest of corns!'

'What? You're a corn that bumbles?'

asked Tangine.

'No, no, I was just being silly with the words,' said King Jamie the Eighth. 'I'm just a bumblicorn . . .'

Tangine looked at him blankly.

'Goodness me,' said the king, buzzing over to Amelia. She instinctively stepped back.

'Oh, I didn't mean to startle you, young vampire creature,' said King Jamie. 'It's just, you seem to be hurt.' He gestured towards her right wing which had a big scratch across it.

Amelia lifted a hand to touch it. '*Ouch*! I must've scraped it when we fell out of the jam jar.' Squashy squeaked and jumped into Amelia's arms to comfort her.

'You fell out of a jam jar?' said King Jamie.

'THAT'S RIGHT,' Florence replied. 'HURT ME LEFT NOSTRIL.'

'Flailing Flamingos!' gasped King Jamie looking concerned. 'You must be tended to!'

'I DUNNO IF I WANNA BE TENDED,' said Florence raising an eyebrow.

'Tended?' said Grimaldi. 'Is that like being stretched?'

'Oh no, dear little reaper,' said the king kindly. 'I think you're getting confused with *ex*-tended. I really think you should all come back to Buggington Palace so that we can tend to your wounds and find you some new clean and dry clothes too.'

'Wait . . . did you say new clothes?'

said Tangine, stepping forward. 'My pride was hurt; does that count?'

'Thank you, King Jamie,' said Amelia carefully. 'But we really need to get back to our Rainbow Ranger leaders. They'll be worried sick when they realise we're gone.'

'He *did* say new clothes!' Tangine said to Amelia pleadingly. 'I mean, look at the state of us! And yellow is *not* my colour.' He patted at the globules of yellow jam clinging to his jumper.

'AND BEING THIS STICKY WOULD MAKE IT 'ARD TO GET VERY FAR RIGHT NOW,' said Florence, lifting a foot which left a trail of jam from her toes to the floor.

Grimaldi looked at Amelia nervously, but didn't say anything.

Suddenly, something creaked in the darkness from the direction of the cave, followed by shuffling and footsteps.

'Okay!' said Amelia, deciding quickly. 'We should get away from here at least . . .' She looked towards the cave nervously. She didn't fancy being swept up again. 'But as soon as we've cleaned up we'll need to find Ricky and Graham so we can get back to our normal size again!'

King Jamie saluted. 'Follow me!'

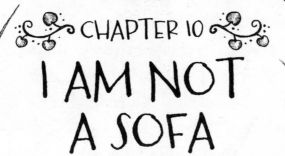

CHAPTER 10
I AM NOT A SOFA

As the friends followed King Jamie through the daisy patch, they answered all his questions about their half-moon holiday and what had led them to the tree. Soon, King Jamie took them up a little spiral staircase carved into a thick flower stem. Amelia hugged Squashy tight.

When the friends reached the top, the tall blades of grass and flowers parted to reveal a whole bug kingdom. All types of bugs were tucked away safely inside hundreds of colourful flower huts. The leaves on the flower

stems acted like little balconies where bugs
had placed deckchairs and sunloungers.
A network of vines, shoots and stalks
connected each flower hut, acting
as sheltered pathways. It was like
nothing Amelia had ever
seen before.

'Welcome to
Buggingtonshire!'
King Jamie said
proudly.

'I'll take you straight to Buggington Palace,
so you can warm up with a nice cup of
Nettle Tea!'

Buggington Palace wasn't hard to spot.
The huge golden honeycomb
structure stretched
higher than all
the flower huts
in the bug
kingdom.

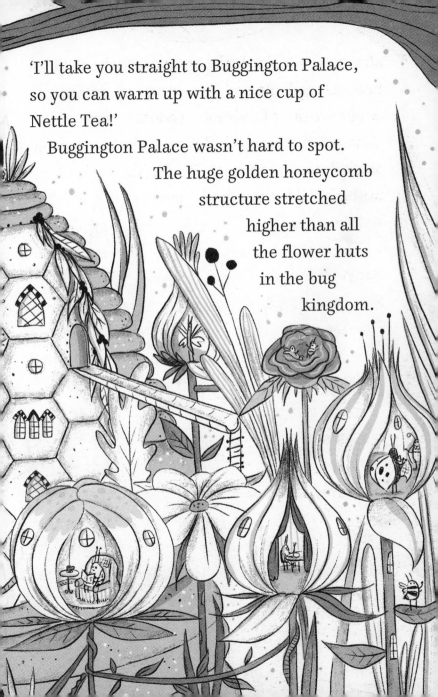

Inside, King Jamie the Eighth led the friends through spongy hallways lined with pictures of knights and past kings and queens. The air and walls were sweet with honey. Squashy leant out of Amelia's arms to lick the walls as they walked past.

'Make yourself at home,' said King Jamie, ushering the friends into a cosy living room, lit by the warm orange glow from a huge fireplace. 'I'll fetch you some dry clothes from the Honey Hall of Garments and have our wonderful maid Madame Flutterby make you a nice warm batch of Nettle Tea. Prickles or no prickles?'

Amelia smiled gratefully and hugged Squashy, whose eyes were now looking in two different directions from all the sugar. 'Um, definitely no prickles for me, thank you.'

'WAIT!' Tangine stepped forward. 'Did you say Honey Hall of Garments? As in a whole *hall* of clothes? Not just a wardrobe, or a

114

room . . . a *hall*?'

'Indeed, Prince Tangerine,' said the king.

'I WANNA PICK AN OUTFIT!' said Florence. 'DO YOU 'AVE CAPES?'

'A whole rack of them,' said King Jamie.

Tangine beamed and Florence rubbed her paws together happily.

'Right this way, both of you!' said the king as he made to leave the room. 'Amelia and Grimaldi, would you like to come and pick something to wear too?'

'No, thank you,' said Amelia feeling the crackling fire warming her toes. 'The fire and some Nettle Tea should do the job.'

'No problem,' said King Jamie. He paused. 'Oh! And you'll meet Denise in due course. . .'

'Denise?' said Grimaldi, as King Jamie left with an excitable Florence and Tangine in tow.

'No idea,' Amelia replied with a shrug. She snuggled up with Squashy and Grimaldi on a big squidgy sofa by the fire whilst Pumpy nibbled on an ornament.

'I think this is quite possibly the comfiest sofa I've ever sat on,' said Amelia as she slowly began to sink into it. Grimaldi had almost disappeared completely.

'Does it feel a little *sticky* to you?' he said, looking slightly concerned.

Amelia shuffled and noticed her skirt slowly peel away from the surface of the sofa leaving a trail of clear goo. 'It can't be goblin slime,' she said poking at it. 'Even goblins are too big for Buggingtonshire, aren't they?'

'It's like snot,' said Grimaldi, wrinkling his nose.

'Sofa . . . sticky . . . goblin . . . *SNOT*?!' came a deep voice from somewhere in the room. 'What do you plan on calling me next?!'

'*Who said that*?' said a bewildered Grimaldi looking around him.

Suddenly the sofa began to move, and with one big DOOOOING, Amelia and

Grimaldi were flung on to the floor.

'Ouch!' Amelia cried, rubbing her bottom. Grimaldi had landed upside down in an ornate vase.

Suddenly, two beady eyes blinked amongst the huge blue blob that Amelia had thought was a sofa, and then a long line appeared for a mouth. The eyes looked Amelia up and down. 'I am NOT a sofa,' it said coldly. 'I am a rare breed of SLUG.'

Amelia raised her eyebrows. 'I think you're going to get along *very* well with our friend Florence.'

CHAPTER 11
THE CURSE OF THE SUGARPLUM TREE

'BOW DOWN FER THE MIGHTY FLO, YER BIG LITTLE MITES!' bellowed Florence as she waltzed into the room where Amelia and Grimaldi were having tea with a massive slug.

Florence was wearing a long red velvet cape with a huge frilly collar and fur trimming. A large golden crown was perched on her head and she held a jewel encrusted staff in one paw which she used to point at whomever she spoke to. 'DON'T I LOOK MAJESTIC?!' she said proudly.

'Who's the beast?' said the slug before taking a dainty sip of Nettle Tea with prickles.

Florence pointed her staff at the slug. 'I AM NOT A BEAST, I'M A RARE BREED OF YETI!' She stepped forward and swished her cape for dramatic effect.

The slug gasped and bowed her head. 'I immediately adore you. I'm Denise by the way – a rare breed of slug.'

Florence grunted and gently poked Denise in the tummy with the staff. 'YOU'RE SO SQUIDGY,' she said. 'PLEASURE TER

MEET YA. SO, WHAT MAKES YOU RARE THEN?'

'My likeness to sofas,' said Denise. 'I'm much bigger and comfier than the average slug. I also have better manners.'

Amelia and Grimaldi chuckled. And Tangine chose that moment to burst into the room looking like an overdressed clown. His hair was sprayed to within an inch of its life and his cheeks were positively glittering. Ruffle upon ruffle bounced around his neck, wrists and ankles and a huge patterned belt kept the whole outfit in its place; which was a good job considering Tangine looked as though he might explode right out of it with joy.

'LOOK AT ME!' he beamed and struck a pose. He walked up to Amelia and put his hands on her shoulders. 'Amelia. I've decided I want to stay here and live in Buggington Palace. It's the *best*. I can be Bug Fashion Guru, and you guys can drink tea ALL DAY! Pumpy can live on a vegetarian diet of petals, which will be good for him. And Squashy . . .' Tangine paused and looked at the little pumpkin who had fallen asleep with his tongue stuck to the honey-coated wall. 'He can just lick the walls.'

Amelia sighed. 'We can't stay here forever, Tangine,' she said softly. We have to get big again and go home. Our family and our friends are in Nocturnia. I miss Mum and

Dad and Wooo.'

'Plus, we can't miss school. We have homework to hand in!' Grimaldi added.

'I DO MISS MY PIT,' said Florence. 'AND MY AUNT'S FAMOUS SLOW WORM SPAG-BOL.'

'I know,' Tangine sighed. 'I do miss Mum's selection of facemasks and Dad's horrifying Hairball Hot-Pot, and my zombie Mummy Maids – especially Helen – it's just that I love that Honey Hall of Garments so much!' He slumped down on Denise.

'Seriously, I am NOT a sofa!' cried the slug.

'Well, when you're *King* of Nocturnia, you can open up your very own Hall of Garments!' said Amelia with a smile. 'It can be your Horrifying Hall of Ghoulish Garments!'

Tangine's eyes lit up.

Amelia looked up at King Jamie. 'I hope you don't think we're being rude. You're being ever so kind, and your palace really is very lovely. It's just . . .' she paused and swallowed hard. 'It's just not home.'

The king smiled. 'I didn't think for one tiny second that you were being rude at all. I'm just sorry you're in such a pickle.'

'So, what exactly happened to you?' asked Denise.

'They ate the glowing fruit from *that* plum tree. . .' said King Jamie, looking concerned.

Denise gasped. 'Oh, the poor darlings have been cursed!'

King Jamie winced. 'I didn't really want to mention that word. There's no need to panic them.'

'TOO LATE,' said Florence.

'*Cursed*?!' shrieked Grimaldi. 'We can't be cursed! Are we going to be tiny forever?'

Amelia felt her belly twist around and around. *Cursed? Surely not?*

'It's what happened to everyone else on this island,' said Denise sadly.

'I thought everyone left the island because it was so small and boring,' said Tangine.

'Nobody ever *left* the island!' Denise said. They're just all *teeny weeny*. All cursed! Like *you*.'

'Over the years, the cursed creatures have adapted to being the size of bugs,' King Jamie explained. 'They've set up a tiny city called Miniopolis on the east side of the island. We trade honey with them once a year in return for their famous Nettle Tea.'

'So, what *is* this curse?' Amelia asked, not sure if she wanted to hear the answer. 'What happened exactly?'

'You've been touched by the Curse of the Sugarplum Tree, I'm afraid,' the king said, turning to Denise. 'Shall I tell the story? Or would you like to, my dearest sluggipops?'

''OLD ON ONE MAJESTIC MINUTE,' said Florence pointing her staff at Denise. 'ARE YOU TWO TOGEVVER? LIKE *TOGEVVER* TOGEVVER?' She made the shape of a heart with her hairy paws.

The king laughed and shimmied up to Denise. 'This is my wife, the Queen of Buggingtonshire!'

'Oh, don't make a big thing out of it, bumblikins,' said Queen Denise.

'Bothering Batwings,' said Grimaldi placing his head in his hands. 'We're welcomed to the palace with open arms and the first thing we do is sit on the queen!'

The king and queen burst out laughing. 'Don't worry about it, tiny death man,' said King Jamie the Eighth. 'I mistake my wife for a sofa more often than not!'

Amelia had thought Queen Denise rather brash to begin with, but the more she got to know her, the more she liked her. Especially when she invited them to sit on her again whilst she told them the story of the Curse of the Sugarplum Tree. 'I do take pride in how utterly comfortable I am, so JUST this once,' the queen said, smiling as Amelia sank into her squidgy exterior.

Queen Denise began. 'Many many *many* years ago, an old gnome called Gretta Grubbikins and the love of her life, a leprechaun called McJiggle, planted a sugarplum seed in their beautiful garden. Over the years, the seed and their love grew, until the most wondrous Sugarplum Tree blossomed. Gretta and McJiggle would dance and jig around the tree every day, humming their own very special tune together.

As the sugarplums grew, they would glow a most wonderful golden colour. The pair shared the delicious plums from the tree with creatures from all over the island. And soon McJiggle even started sailing over to the Dazzling Docks every morning to sell them all over the Kingdom of the Light. The creatures LOVED them. Each night he would use the glow of the Sugarplum Tree to sail home safely to his beloved Gretta Grubbikins.'

Florence sniffed. 'THIS IS A LOVELY STORY SO FAR,' she said wiping an eye.

'BUT . . .' said Queen Denise.

'OH,' Florence grunted. 'I DON'T LIKE THE SOUND OF THAT *BUT*. . .'

CHAPTER 12
THE NECTAR CARRIAGE

'One night,' Queen Denise continued. 'McJiggle did not return home. Gretta waited and waited, but morning came and still there was no sign of him.'

'No sign . . .' Amelia murmured to herself, remembering the scribbles covering the cave walls. 'Wait! Was that *Gretta Grubbikins* inside the cave?'

King Jamie nodded. 'Most probably. She's been hiding away in that cave for years now. She never comes out.'

Denise nodded sadly. 'So every night that passed, the lonelier Gretta grew. And as the years went by, the Sugarplum Tree was Gretta Grubbikin's only reminder of her beloved McJiggle.

'And in her sadness, she no longer wished to share the sugarplums with anyone else until McJiggle came home. But the creatures of the island loved the fruit so much, they would still sneak into the garden to pick them.

'Before hiding herself away for good, Gretta cursed the tree. This curse meant that anyone who ate a sugarplum from the tree would shrink to the size of a sugarplum themselves. Then they would never be able to pick from the tree again.

'One by one, the creatures of the island seemed to disappear and soon enough, Sugarplum Island appeared to be deserted.'

'And that's the story of the Sugarplum Curse,' said King Jamie the Eighth, grimacing. 'I'm sorry it's not better news for you all.'

'I think that every day McJiggle didn't come back Gretta Grubbikins recorded it on the walls of her cave,' said Amelia.

'She always lived in the hope that McJiggle would return,' said Denise. 'Wouldn't you if someone you loved had disappeared?'

'Yes,' said Tangine sadly. And Amelia realised that he was thinking of his own mum who had been missing for years before Amelia, Tangine and the gang had rescued her from a unicorn prison. Amelia gave his hand a reassuring squeeze. 'If we can free your mum, Tangine, then we must be able to free ourselves from this curse, *somehow*!'

'There *must* be a way to break it,' Grimaldi agreed hopefully. 'All curses can be broken, right?'

'Well, yes dear,' said Queen Denise. 'But I think the only way to break the curse would be if McJiggle came back, and he was lost to the sea – lost forever.'

'WELL 'OW ABOUT WE GO BACK TO THE
CAVE AND TALK TO GRETTA?' said Florence.
'TELL 'ER THAT CURSING AIN'T GONNA
MAKE 'ER FEEL BETTER.'

'I don't think it's quite that easy, fair yeti,'
said King Jamie kindly.

'Wait!' Amelia suddenly piped up. 'Maybe,
just maybe, we could *wish* ourselves big again
at the Wishing Well of Well Wishes back in
the Kingdom of the Light!'

'OOO, THAT'S A GOOD IDEA, AMELIA!'
said Florence looking impressed. 'I KNEW
YOU'D COME UP WIV AN ANSWER – YOU
ALWAYS DO.' She smiled and put a big hairy
arm around Amelia's shoulders.

'It's a strong curse,' said King Jamie. 'But
a valiant idea and worth a try indeed!'

'We'll need to reach Ricky and Graham so
they can take us back to the Wishing Well.

But I still don't know how we're going to reach them while we're this small' said Amelia, feeling so frustrated by it all.

'Where is your campsite?' asked King Jamie the Eighth.

'It's on the beach, facing the Dazzling Docks,' Amelia replied.

'Ah, the west of the island,' said King Jamie. 'I can take you there in my special Nectar Carriage.'

'Really? That would be amazing. You're being so kind to us, King Jamie,' said Amelia. 'Are you sure you don't mind?'

King Jamie smiled and stood up straight. 'You are guests in my home. As king, I strive to do good for the community and help others. You are lost and in need of help and I can do my very best to provide that help.'

'Truth is, he loves ANY excuse to use his shiny new Nectar Carriage!' said Denise,

139

with one raised eyebrow.

Amelia giggled.

King Jamie gave his wife an affectionate nudge. 'The cheek of it!' he said. 'That may be a *very* tiny part of it. But what's the point of a king who does nothing but sit on his throne and look pretty?'

'When I'm King of Nocturnia, I definitely plan to sit on my throne and look pretty,' said Tangine, admiring his reflection in a long mirror on the wall.

'But if I can be even half the king you are, King Jamie, I'll know I'm doing something right.'

Both King Jamie and Tangine bowed to one another.

'And I wouldn't mind a unicorn horn either,' Tangine added.

CHAPTER 13
OI, KEVIN!

The sleigh-style carriage (made entirely of solid honeycomb) zipped through the air silently with Amelia and her friends tucked inside safe and sound. King Jamie sat on a small ledge at the front of the carriage holding on to reins, which were attached to a bustle of harnessed fireflies. Their bright glow lit their way through the night sky.

Pumpy was wriggling around on Tangine's lap trying to catch the breeze in his mouth.

'May I ask that the big pumpkin be kept as still as possible please?' King Jamie called back from the driver's seat. 'We've never flown this fast before and I don't want anyone to fall!'

Florence scooped Pumpy up with one paw and wedged him under her arm, much to the pumpkin's dismay. "EE AIN'T GOING NOWHERE NOW.'

As the flying carriage approached the west of the island, tiny beacons of light became visible from around the Rainbow Ranger campsite. The lights were moving, heading towards the sea. As the Nectar Carriage drew closer, Amelia noticed the Rainbow Rangers holding torches and climbing into their boats, including Ricky and Graham.

'Wait a minute,' said Amelia feeling like a brick had fallen into her stomach. 'They're leaving!'

'*What*?!' Grimaldi shrieked. 'They can't leave! Ricky and Graham will be gone and we'll have no way of getting big again. We'll be stuck here forever!'

'We need to hurry!' said Amelia, feeling

panic wash over her.

'Which of those creatures are Ricky and Graham?' asked King Jamie.

'THOSE BIG UNICORNS THERE!' said Florence pointing towards them.

'Okay, hold on tight!' yelled King Jamie. '*FASTER!*' he commanded the fireflies, guiding them downwards at top speed.

Everything appeared to blur as the carriage whizzed through the air faster and faster, making Amelia's eyes water. The fireflies' wings were flapping so quickly, it looked as if they weren't moving at all. Then, close to the ground, just as they had almost reached Ricky and Graham, a high pitched SQUEEEEEEEEEEEEEEEAK was heard.

One of the fireflies floundered in mid-air and the Nectar Carriage swerved, spinning high into the air as the frantic insects reared off course.

Amelia gasped as King Jamie went tumbling on to the sand below.

Florence clambered to the front of the carriage and grabbed the reins.

'Can anyone see King Jamie?' Amelia cried, leaning as far over the side as she dared.

Her head spun as she looked down from high up. But, sure enough, there on the sand, with his crown knocked off, lay the royal bumblicorn.

Just a few metres away, the Rainbow Rangers were pushing their boats into the water and, for a moment, Amelia didn't know what to do. If they went back to help King Jamie the boats would be gone – and the gang would have lost their chance to get home.

But really there was no choice.

'We have to go back and make sure that King Jamie is okay!' said Amelia, climbing into the seat next to Florence and taking one of the reins.

'But I don't *want* to be small forever!' Tangine protested from the back.

'Tangine . . . King Jamie helped us,' Amelia gently reminded her friend. 'We have to help him!'

Tangine nodded, looking a little bit ashamed.

'BAAAAAACK!' Florence bellowed at the fireflies, as she and Amelia pulled tightly on the reins – and away from the Rainbow Rangers.

When they landed on the sand they found King Jamie with his legs up in the air and his bumblicorn horn stuck in the sand.

'Is . . . is he dead?!' said Grimaldi nervously.

'Not quite.' King Jamie the Eighth opened his eyes slowly and weakly waved up at the concerned faces above him. 'But you must go! Fly on, young Nocturnian friends!'

'THANK THE GRAVE!' cried Florence. 'LET'S GO!'

But when Amelia and her friends looked up, all they could see were the silhouettes of little boats bobbing away towards the horizon.

It was too late.

They were in a very sticky situation indeed.

And this time it had nothing to do with jam.

'They've gone,' Grimaldi's little voice broke through the shocked silence.

Amelia couldn't speak. She clutched Squashy to her tightly as tears dripped down her face.

'I am so sorry,' said King Jamie. 'I shall renounce my crown straight away and give it to that young one-eyed man over there.'

Florence sighed sadly. 'NO, YOU DON'T 'AV TO DO THAT, KING JAM–' She stopped. 'ER, WHAT? WHAT *YOUNG MAN*?'

Everyone looked up to see Kevin the Cyclops running towards the shore, dragging a small boat behind him. 'Wait for meeeeee!'

Amelia jumped into action. 'King Jamie, can we borrow your carriage to fly over to that cyclops please?'

'Of course!' the royal bumblicorn replied looking very relieved. 'And may all the luck of

Buggintonshire be with you!'

The Nectar Carriage veered up towards Kevin, their very last hope of being big again.

The cyclops climbed into the boat and Amelia shouted as loud as she could. 'KEVIN! *HEY KEVIN*! IT'S ME, AMELIA, AND EVERYONE ELSE! WE'RE HERE!'

But Kevin couldn't hear her. He picked up his oars.

The carriage drew closer.

Kevin seemed to sense something near his head and sat up a little straighter.

'OI, KEVIN!' Florence yelled. She had a much louder voice than Amelia.

'He can't hear us!' Amelia shouted. 'We need to get in front of his eye!'

Florence managed to steer the Nectar Carriage back round to face Kevin.

'*KEVIIIIIIIIIN*!' they shouted again as they flew towards his face to get his attention.

Everyone waved their arms about.

Kevin's one eye twitched. He put down an oar and slowly lifted a hand up in the air. He must have recognised them!

'*ARGH! BLASTED BUGS!*' His hand swatted the carriage away.

The Nectar Carriage went crashing towards the Sea of Sparkles. The fireflies scattered and flew away in different directions.

Amelia saw King Jamie flying nearby. He tried to reach out and grab her and her friends, but was just out of reach.

The stars in the sky above disappeared from her view. King Jamie was but a distant buzz and the last things she saw were the flickering glow of the fireflies as she sank deeper and deeper into the water.

CHAPTER 14
CORAL JUICE

'You okay honey?'

Amelia felt something nudge her shoulder softly.

She slowly opened her eyes. She felt dizzy.

'Easy does it, lovely one,' said a voice.

Amelia was lying on something soft and kind of fluffy. As she yawned, a big bubble of water rose from her mouth. She felt as if she was moving in slow motion. Everything seemed wibbly wobbly, like she was underwater.

And then as everything came into focus she realised . . . she *was* underwater!

'Thank the oysters you're okay!' said the voice again.

Amelia looked to her side to see a friendly looking creature with caramel skin, short, squiggly white hair and big eyes staring straight at her.

'I'm Nurse Bubble!' said the creature. 'How are you feeling, Amelia?'

Amelia winced as she sat up a bit too fast, her wing still hurting. 'Where am I? Where are my friends? And Squashy? Is he okay?!'

Nurse Bubble placed a hand gently on Amelia's shoulder. 'It's okay, your friends are well, tucked up nice and cosy too, here in the Oyster Infirmary in the Kingdom of Aquatica! Grimaldi, Florence the rare fluffy one and Prince Tangine are all together! And your little pumpkin and his large pumpkin friend are busy munching on a bowl of Kelp Krispies.'

Amelia took a deep breath. Her thoughts slowly unjumbled and she remembered what had happened. Her heart sunk – because of her decision they had missed the boat. She knew they had done the right thing saving King Jamie but she couldn't believe they weren't on their way to the Wishing Well of Well Wishes.

Amelia leant back against the pillow and looked around. The scene before her was quite spectacular. Clusters of colourful sea plants of all shapes and sizes swayed lightly in the current, and small creatures with tails, fins and googly eyes swam in and out of them.

Stretching as far as the eye could see were bobbly huts covered in brightly-coloured lichen and pretty flowers. Curly weed-like plants weaved themselves around pebbles and every so often, bursts of rainbow bubbles would erupt from pointy rocks.

'It's pretty, isn't it?' said the nurse, swishing her glimmering yellow fishtail. She gave a big friendly smile revealing two big fangs.

Amelia gasped.

'Why, you look a little alarmed,' said Nurse Bubble as she turned around and plumped up Amelia's pillow. 'Ooooh, of course! You've probably never seen a mer-pire before, have you? But look!' Nurse Bubble clapped her hands. 'Here are your friends to see you! I would prepare yourself a little, Amelia Fang!'

'Why do I –?' But Amelia stopped mid-sentence, staring in amazement as a star-shaped Squashy, with suckers on each of his five-pointed arms, came bobbing through the water to Amelia's bed.

He was followed by a concerned looking Grimaldi who had a wispy black fishtail.

Pumpy soon appeared, munching on something red. He had a big curly seahorse tail. It was a very strange sight indeed.

Nurse Bubble rushed over and removed the red thing from his mouth. It turned out it wasn't food at all, it was another nurse; who happened to be a very distressed looking crab.

'Sorry about that, Brenda,' said Nurse Bubble as Brenda huffed and scurried away.

'FINK I LOOK QUITE GOOD WIF A TAIL!' bellowed Florence swimming in and swishing her big fluffy tail in circles creating a mini whirlpool.

'At least you GOT a tail!' said a familiar voice. Tangine swam over. 'Do NOT laugh.' He folded his arms and frowned. Instead of a fishtail, Tangine had eight long tentacles. 'These do NOT suit my complexion!'

Amelia chuckled and adjusted her blankets. That's when she saw it. Instead of a pair of legs, she had a fishtail.

'Gaaaaaaaaaaah!'

'Coral Juice!' the mer-pire nurse gently ordered a shocked Amelia, brandishing a flask in her face. 'It'll make you feel much better. And, you know, it's what gave you all the ability to swim and breathe underwater!'

Suddenly a jolly voice boomed '*Nurse Bubble*! Me ol' whipper snapper! I hear we've some new patients in need of my silliness.'

'Our new patients are awake and are certainly in need of your love and care!' said Nurse Bubble giving a small and old mer-creature a big hug.

'Aye, jolly good, jolly good,' he replied. He was very wrinkly with a long white beard and long hair. He had a green glittery fishtail and wore an apron which was covered in paint splatters. His face was a kind one with rosy cheeks and a mischievous smile. 'I'm Mr Grubs, resident artist, entertainer, smile-maker and General Takerer-Carerer of the injured. I'm here to make you laugh and help heal those wounds.' He did a little jig and span on the spot.

Nurse Bubble introduced the friends to Mr Grubs. 'This is Amelia, Florence, Grimaldi and Tangine.'

Tangine tried to hold out a royal tentacle to be greeted by Mr Grub, but ended up in one big knot.

'They're creatures from the Land Above. Took a terrible fall about an hour ago,' said the nurse.

An hour ago?! thought Amelia. Ricky, Graham and the Rainbow Rangers would definitely be back in the Kingdom of the Light by now – probably on their way back to Nocturnia. How would they ever get back now?

'You look sad, Amelia. What's wrong?' Nurse Bubble asked gently.

Amelia shuffled uncomfortably. 'It's just, um, I'm sorry, Nurse Bubble. But we really need to get back home to reverse a curse – we need to get ourselves big again. I just don't know how we're going to do it. . .'

The others all looked worried too. Tangine gave Florence's hairy hand a reassuring squeeze and Squashy gave Amelia's fishtail a comforting lick.

'A curse, you say?' Nurse Bubble's already huge eyes widened and she glanced at Mr Grub quickly, before shaking her head as if dismissing a thought. 'Well, that does explain why you were the size of my hand when I found you. The trusty Coral Juice made you bigger,' she said.

'That stuff's a doozy!' chuckled Mr Grubs.

'Wait,' said Grimaldi, the big black holes of his eyes as big as Nurse Bubble's. 'Does that mean we're *not* tiny anymore?! And the curse is broken?'

Amelia felt an ounce of hope explode inside her chest and Florence snorted in shock.

'Oh, honey, I'm sorry,' said Bubble. 'I'm afraid not. You'll return to your tiny size the minute you're back on dry land. The Coral Juice only works underwater.'

Amelia sighed and watched as a huge manta-ray dragon floated past the window making a low rumbling WAAAAAAAAAAAAAAOOOOOOOOOOOOOOOOOOAAAAAAAAA sound.

'We do appreciate you saving our lives, Nurse Bubble. But we really need to go now.' Amelia tried to get up and swim, but Nurse Bubble put a hand gently on her shoulder and guided her back into the shell bed.

'I think you should rest up a bit before you go anywhere,' said Nurse Bubble with concern. 'You've quite a few bumps and bruises. And it's the middle of the night, so you'll need your sleep. Myself and Mr Grubs here will make you feel right at home'

'It's okay, we're not tired,' said Amelia, easing herself out of the shell bed.

'Well, that's the perfect excuse for some painting then! A nice bit of art is one of the best ways to relax!' I'll go fetch my paints and some paper!' said Mr Grubs, swimming off humming to himself.

Amelia gasped. 'It's that tune again!'

CHAPTER 15
THE TIDDLYPIPS WING

Florence, Tangine and Grimaldi piled on to Amelia's shell bed with Squashy and Pumpy pa-doinging and PA-DOOFING behind them. 'THIS PLACE IS CRAZY,' said Florence. 'I KNOW WE NEED TO GET HOME SOON BUT I NEVA FORT I'D SEE THE DAY WHEN I'D GET TURNED INTO A MER-YETI!'

'I bet nobody's seen mer-death before!' giggled Grimaldi.

But Amelia was too distracted by what she'd just heard to think of anything else. 'Guys! I heard that tune again! I heard it when I was being pushed along in the boat and won the race, and it's the same tune Gretta Grubbikins was humming in the cave.'

'Maybe it's just a popular song that creatures sing around here,' said Grimaldi.

'Maybe . . .' said Amelia. 'I don't know. But I can't help feeling like it means something more.'

'WHAT D'YA MEAN?' said Florence, looking doubtful.

'I've just been wondering *how* someone who lives under the sea would be humming the *exact* same tune as someone who hides away in a cave . . .'

Nurse Bubble swam merrily into the room to refill their flasks of Coral Juice.

'Nurse Bubble,' said Amelia. 'Who exactly *is* Mr Grubs?'

'Why, he's the loveliest merma-chaun in the Kingdom of Aquatica!' she beamed.

'He did admire my brand-new tentacles,'

agreed Tangine, waving one round grandly

Grimaldi giggled.

'But was he *born* here?' asked Amelia, as Squashy snuggled into the shell next to her.

'No . . .' said Nurse Bubble, smiling at Amelia curiously. 'He's from the Land Above. My mother was working here at the Oyster Infirmary many years ago when they found him. He had a massive bump on his head and when he eventually woke up, he couldn't remember anything about, well, *anything*! Since he couldn't even remember his name, he decided to call himself *Mr Grubs*! It was the first thing that popped into his head.'

Nurse Bubble sat Amelia up gently and straightened her covers. 'He's such a lovely chap – when I was a little mer-pire, I used to visit Mr Grubs while my mother worked long shifts, and he'd tell me jokes and paint me wonderful pictures, always humming his little song.'

Amelia could feel Nurse Bubble's fondness for Mr Grubs as if it were a big warm blanket of love.

'Do you know,' Nurse Bubbles continued, 'that whenever he's not helping around the hospital, he's at the water's surface helping anyone crossing the water from here to Sugarplum Island.'

Suddenly Amelia remembered how her little boat seemingly sailed itself across the Sea of Sparkles. *It must have been Mr Grubs!* That's when she first heard him humming that tune. But what kept him going back and forth from here to Sugarplum Island?

'Is there something on your mind little vampire?' Nurse Bubble asked Amelia, tipping her head to one side.

But before Amelia could ask anything, she was stopped by the sound of Tangine calling urgently.

'*Ameeeeeeeelia*!'

Where was he? Amelia hadn't realised he'd even left the room.

'Tangine?' she called. 'Are you okay?'

A few tentacles poked out from the open

doorway, gesturing for Amelia to follow.

'He must be in the Tiddlypips Wing,' said Nurse Bubble, looking slightly confused. 'That's where the baby sea creatures sleep so best keep it *hush hush*!'

'GET OUT THE BABY ROOM, YOU BIG FRUIT,' said Florence swimming over to collect Tangine by the tentacle. Then she stopped. 'OH, BUT SPEAKING OF FRUIT . . .'

Amelia swam towards the Tiddlypips Wing.

A curious Grimaldi followed. As they swam round the corner, they passed tiny mer-pires, octo-wolves, uni-fish, vampire-squid and other bizarre baby underwater creatures fast asleep in teeny weeny shells. But then they looked up. There in front of them was a huge mural that covered the entire wall on one side of the room. And it showed something they had seen before.

'It's the Sugarplum Tree,' Amelia

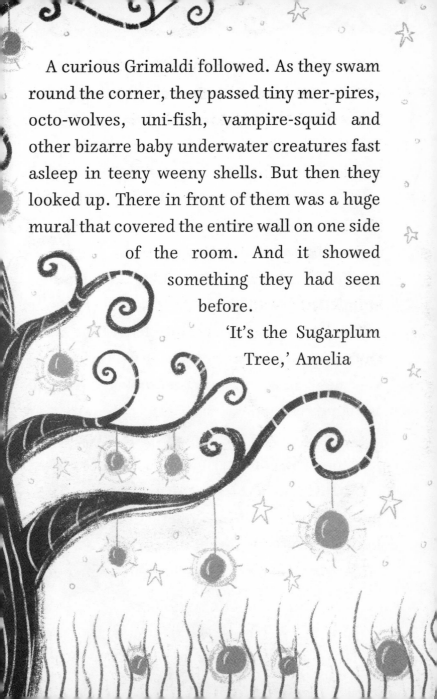

said quietly. 'The only thing the gnome, Gretta *Grub*bikins, had left of her beloved leprechaun, McJiggle, before he went missing, sailing plums to the mainland.'

'MR GRUB!' cried Nurse Bubble. 'I think you might have something there, little vampire!'

Amelia nodded excitedly.

'*What*?! I demand to know what everyone is wondering? And why haven't they told me when I am the prince and clearly the most important person here?' Tangine huffed, waving his many tentacles around indignantly.

Grimaldi's eyes widened as it dawned on him too. 'Grubbikins ... Grub ... Mr *Grub* ...'

'MCJIGGLE!' Florence bellowed. Then quickly put her hands over her mouth as a baby mer-pire stirred in the corner.

'*Creeping corals*!' Nurse Bubbles whispered

in excitement. 'Can it be we *finally* know where Mr Grubs came from?'

Amelia grinned, feeling like a light inside her had pinged on.

'Hold on,' said Tangine as the penny finally dropped. 'Now, let's say Mr Grubs *is* McJiggle, Gretta's one true love, well, if it's anything like all the Kingdom of the Light fairy-tale books I've read, then maybe just maybe . . .'

'OH MY FLIPPERS, GET ON WIV IT!' groaned Florence.

Tangine shot her a glare, then flourished his tentacles. 'What I was saying before I was rudely interrupted was MAYBE True Love's Kiss could break the curse? *Our* curse?'

'I AIN'T KISSING NO ONE,' said Florence folding her arms.

'Ummm . . . I don't think he meant you,' Grimaldi added.

'Yes Tangine!' Amelia cried. For the first

time since they'd been at the Oyster Infirmary, she felt much much better. She twirled around in the water. 'If we reunite Gretta with McJiggle, then surely she'll lift the curse and we can be big again!'

CHAPTER 16

IT'S ALL COMING BACK TO 'IM!

That familiar tune filled the Oyster Infirmary and Mr Grubs came swimming into the main room with his arms full to the brim with art materials.

Amelia poked her head out from the entrance of the Tiddlypips Wing.

'Whatch'ya all doing in there?' said Mr Grubs as he lay out some paper. 'I've got some arty treats here for you!'

'That tune you were humming . . .' said Amelia, approaching Mr Grubs, as her friends swam in behind her. She felt oddly nervous and was glad they were all there together.

'I think I've heard it somewhere before.'

Mr Grubs looked at Amelia and lowered his glasses. 'Really?' he said furrowing his brows. 'How does a wee lass like you know a funny tune like that then? It's always in my head. Not sure where it came from.'

'That's just it,' said Amelia. 'I think I *may* know where it comes from. I'm not one hundred per cent sure, but it's possible . . . well, if my feeling is right . . .'

'We might have figured out who you really are!' said Nurse Bubble, rushing over.

Mr Grubs took his glasses off. 'Bubble dear, you've been working a long shift, perhaps it's break time?'

Nurse Bubble took his hands gently. 'No, Mr Grubs. The tree you painted in the Tiddlypips Wing . . . Well, Amelia and her friends say they've seen that tree before. On Sugarplum Island – in the Land Above.'

'Sugarplum Island?' said Mr Grubs, raising an eyebrow.

'There's a gnome that lives there,' said Amelia. 'Years ago, a leprechaun she loved very much disappeared. His name was McJiggle and her name is Gretta Grubbikins.'

Mr Grubs stared at Amelia for a second, then plopped down on the edge of one of the shell beds.

'Gretta Grubbikins . . .' he muttered under his breath, like he was searching in the depths of his mind. 'I feel like I know that name.' Mr Grubs put a hand to his chest. 'But I'm afraid I can't remember. I'm sorry.' He bowed his head in sadness.

The friends floated in silence.

'Maybe he's not McJiggle after all,' said Grimaldi quietly.

But then Amelia started humming a tune. The same tune she'd heard when her little boat was pushed along the water. The same tune Gretta had hummed in the cave. The same tune Mr Grubs had been humming earlier on.

Mr Grubs looked at her. He began to hum along. Mr Grubs closed his eyes and then he stopped humming and whispered gently. 'Gretta. My beloved Gretta Grubbikins.' His eyes began to well up. 'It's all coming back to me!'

'IT'S ALL COMING BACK TO 'IM!' said Florence, waving her tail around and slapping Grimaldi smack bang in the middle of the eyes. A baby bat-fish began to cry.

'And I am McJiggle Grubbikins!' declared the mer-machaun, delightedly. He rose and gave a little jig surrounding himself in small bubbles. 'I remember who I am! I am McJiggle and I live on Sugarplum Island with my beloved Gretta!'

'Oh, thank the grave,' said Tangine adjusting his knotted tentacles. 'Maybe *you* can tell her to stop cursing everyone.'

'What do you mean?' said McJiggle, looking a little confused.

Amelia blushed. 'Hmmm, well, the thing is, Gretta was so upset about losing you that she cursed the tree, so anyone who ate from it shrunk to the size of a sugarplum. The tree was her only reminder of you and she didn't want anyone touching it after you'd gone.'

McJiggle looked a little embarrassed. 'Oh, well that's no good at all!'

'Oh, honey! Isn't that lovely?!' said Bubble, spinning on the spot. 'To have someone love you so much, they're willing to CURSE others to keep the memory of you alive!'

McJiggle sighed and took Bubble's hands in his. 'My dear, dear Bubble. You have shown me nothing but love and kindness all the years

I've lived here. I don't know how to thank you.'

Nurse Bubble hugged him tight. 'Mr Gr– I mean, *McJiggle*. Actually, you'll always be Mr Grubs to me.' She smiled. 'I truly am delighted that you remember who you really are. You don't need to thank me at all. You have been a dear friend to me since I was a tiny mer-pire, and even though I'm going to miss you more than you'll ever know, you will never, ever be forgotten here.'

McJiggle chuckled. 'Just don't miss me so much that you put a crazy curse on anyone, eh?'

Amelia and her friends looked at each other unsure how to react. Then they all burst out laughing.

'GROUP HUUUUG!' yelled Florence and dragged everyone into her furry embrace.

'Well, I guess you should head to the shore,' said Nurse Bubble once she'd reluctantly stepped back from the wonderful yeti hug. 'You need to get back to your Gretta!'

'Well, this is goodbye,' said Nurse Bubble a few minutes later. 'Once you set foot, or should I say, *fin* on land, the Coral Juice will wear off. You'll soon have your normal bodies and return to the tiny size you were before.'

Amelia sighed. She'd got used to being big again – even if she did have a tail!

'It's okay,' grinned McJiggle. 'You'll be in good hands,' he said, holding out his own. 'I'm sure there'll be enough room on me ol' wrinkly palms to carry you lot when we're back on shore.'

'Oh definitely,' Nurse Bubble chuckled. 'They were teeny weeny and super cute when I found them.'

'Well, that goes without saying,' said Tangine, fluttering his eyes.

Nurse Bubble burst out laughing. Amelia, Florence, Grimaldi and Tangine all gave Nurse Bubble one last hug goodbye, before she gave Squashy and Pumpy some extra Kelp Krispies to munch on.

McJiggle was last to say farewell.

'At least I know I'll be in good hands if I ever have a boating mishap again.' He winked. 'I will never forget what you have done for me.'

Nurse Bubble took a deep breath. 'Well, I've decided to rename the Oyster Infirmary,' she said with a grin. 'If you ever find yourself toppling into the sea again, you might well end up in the Jigglygrubs Infirmary.'

The friends burst out laughing.

Nurse Bubble gave a little twirl and waved. 'Goodbye my friends from the Land Above!' And she disappeared into the depths of the Sea of Sparkles.

CHAPTER 17
THE TINGLE

The sun shone brightly on the horizon as Amelia opened her eyes. Her clothes were wet and a now GIANT McJiggle was sprawled out on the sand next to her. She'd almost forgotten how small the curse had made them. Squashy and Pumpy were rolling around in a pile of crispy purple seaweed nearby.

'My hair is an utter MESS!' said Tangine, sitting a little further away and trying to pat down the glittery frizz. 'Whoever said sea salt was good for texture was SO WRONG.'

McJiggle stretched his legs out. 'Shuddering sugarplums,' he said. 'I haven't used these in years!' He wiggled his toes. 'Amelia? Amelia's friends whose names escape me? I know there was a fluffy one and one with wings . . . and a small deathly one. Where are you?'

'McJiggle!' Amelia called as loudly as possible in her tiny voice.

The old leprechaun looked around him confused.

'Down here!' yelled Amelia waving her arms. 'Guys, I need your help getting his attention, he can't hear us!'

'*Wooooooooooooo, McJiggle*! *Over here*!' cried Grimaldi.

'*Hellooooooo*!' called Tangine.

Florence climbed up to McJiggle's ear. 'YO! JOLLYJIGGLES!' she bellowed. This seemed to do the trick.

'Oh, my!' said McJiggle, turning his head from where he lay and spotting a tiny Amelia, Florence, Grimaldi and Tangine. 'You mentioned the curse made you small, but I didn't realise quite how small!'

'YEAH, YOU CAN FANK GRETTA FOR THAT,' said Florence.

'Ah my apologies, dark little creatures of Nocturnia.' McJiggle scooped the little friends up in his wrinkly hands.

'COME ON THEN MCDOOGLE,' said Florence, softening. 'LET'S GET YOU 'OME SO WE CAN BREAK THIS CURSE!'

Amelia looked up at McJiggle. 'Are you ready?' she said softly. He closed his eyes and took in a deep breath. Then he opened his eyes and looked towards the top of the mountain.

'I'm coming home, Gretta.'

The Sugarplum Tree was still glowing even in the morning sunlight.

McJiggle stood at the edge of the garden holding Amelia, Florence, Grimaldi, Tangine and the pumpkins safely in his hands.

'I . . .' he began, then gulped. 'I don't know what to say. It's been so long. What if Gretta doesn't recognise me or thinks I'm too old and wrinkly now?'

'DON'T WORRY MCJIGGUMS. I'M SURE GRETTA'S GOT A FEW WRINKLES 'ERSELF, DON'T YOU WORRY,' said Florence.

'I can recommend you a great eyelid cream,' said Tangine.

Florence elbowed him. 'NO ONE'S INTERESTED IN YOUR SILLY EYELID CREAM,' she said.

Amelia stood up and looked McJiggle in the eyes. 'Of course Gretta will recognise you! She loves you!'

'Enough to curse an island,' said Grimaldi with a nod.

"If you're not sure what to say, why don't you hum?' suggested Amelia.

McJiggle smiled. 'I think that's a wonderful idea,' he said, placing Amelia and her friends down carefully on to a low branch of the Sugarplum Tree. 'Wish me luck,' he said and then sat down beneath the tree, closed his eyes and began to hum his and Gretta's tune. Squashy waggled his stalk in time with the tune and a light breeze caused a few sugarplums to fall to the ground.

But there was no sign of Gretta. Amelia held on to Grimaldi's hand tightly.

'Why isn't she coming?' asked Grimaldi.

McJiggle looked over at Amelia. He looked

heartbroken. Amelia began to feel hopeless.

But then McJiggle hummed again and this time louder and with passion. He stood up and started to walk towards the cave as the tune resonated through the leaves. Even the sugarplums seemed to glow a bit brighter.

And that's when Amelia felt Florence bump her shoulder. 'HEADS UP!' she said.

Amelia looked up and saw movement in the cave entrance at the end of the garden. McJiggle walked towards the cave, humming all the time – and soon instead of one voice, there were two, as Gretta Grubbikins emerged from the darkness of her cave for the first time in years.

She walked across the garden slowly, using a wooden stick to support her. She stopped in front of McJiggle.

'It can't be . . .' Gretta breathed.

'My Gretta,' McJiggle whispered as he took

her hand in his.

Tangine sniffed.

'AWW, YOU ALL 'MOTIONAL, TANGINE?' said Florence putting a big hairy arm around Tangine's shoulders.

'No!' said Tangine defensively, whilst wiping his eyes. 'YOU'RE emotional.'

'Does anyone feel a bit tingly?' said Grimaldi scratching his arms.

'I waited for you every day and every night,' Gretta said to McJiggle. 'I didn't want to believe you were gone. But after years of waiting, I'd lost hope. I never thought I'd ever see you again!'

And with that, Gretta hugged McJiggle so tightly, it looked as though she may squeeze the life right out of him.

'OKAY, I FEEL THAT NOW,' said Florence, wincing. She shuffled and wriggled. 'MOVE UP, TANGINE!'

'I can't!' Tangine snapped. 'Your huge

200

bottom is in the way! Hey, Amelia, can't you move up?'

'There's no room!' she said as Grimaldi squealed. 'I'm going to fall off! Stop pushing!'

And then there was a SNAP as the branch gave way beneath them.

CHAPTER 18

BE TINY AND BRAVE

Amelia, Florence, Tangine, Grimaldi and the pumpkins fell to the floor. Amelia braced herself for a very sore bottom but soon realised they hadn't actually fallen very far.

They were a normal size once again!

McJiggle, still hugging Gretta, gasped.

'The curse has been broken!' said Amelia

'AN SO AV OUR BACKS!', moaned Florence.

Gretta gazed at McJiggle. 'I swore the curse would break if you came back to me.'

'Ah, yes,' the leprechaun smiled. 'I hear you've made quite an impact on this island . . .'

Gretta blushed. 'They were picking our plums!' Then she softened. 'I'm sorry. All I had left of you was the Sugarplum Tree.'

'S'ALRIGHT,' Florence cut in. 'GUESS WIFFOUT THE CURSE WE WOULD NEVA 'AVE FOUND MCJIGGLY, EH?!'

Gretta giggled. 'I don't know how to thank you for bringing my McJiggle back,' she said sincerely.

'Perhaps by NOT sweeping us up and chucking us out into the rain?' said Tangine.

'*Tangine*!' Amelia hissed, putting her head in her hands.

Gretta's eyes widened. 'Oh deary dear,' she said. 'My eyes aren't too great these days. I did *think* it was a little odd that jam jar fell over and smashed!'

Everybody laughed before the sound of hooves and rustling was heard in some nearby trees. Suddenly, two flustered looking unicorns appeared.

'Ricky, Graham!' said Amelia running over to them. 'We thought you'd left!'

'Galloping Gooseberries!' said Ricky as Amelia threw her arms around him. 'Thank the stars you're safe! We'd all sailed round to the other side of the island to find you when some King corn-bum-number-eight–'

'He's a *bum-bleeee-corn* actually,' Graham corrected him.

Ricky frowned. 'Yes, that's what he said. Anyway, the king-baggicorn came along with a WHOLE kingdom's worth of bugs and surrounded us!'

'Ricky thought they were gonna attack us,' said Graham rolling his eyes.

'You thought it too! And STOP interrupting my story!' said Ricky defensively. 'But anyway, it was only to get our attention, and he told us what had happened – that you'd fallen into the sea! We were beside ourselves! Jamie the bumbaborn guided us here to find a gnome named Gretta who'd done a curse or somefink.'

'You said it wrong again, Ricky,' said Graham. 'King Jamie is a bumpy-corn!'

'Bumblicorn,' said a very small, but familiar voice. 'But you can just call me King Jamie.

And it's really not worth squabbling over.'

The Nectar Carriage bobbed up and down in the air. Queen Denise was sitting in the back fanning herself. 'Coo-eee!' she called happily.

'KING JAMIE!' said Amelia and her friends in unison.

'I'm so glad you're okay,' he said. 'What happened?'

'Don't worry!' said Amelia with a grin.

'We were taken care of by a mer-pire called Nurse Bubble – there's a whole other kingdom under the Sea of Sparkles!'

'Really? I never knew about that!' said the bumblicorn.

'It's where we found McJiggle! He'd been living under the sea all this time,' said Amelia.

The king gasped. 'And THAT'S why you're big again! And you're not the only ones. The curse has been broken! There are creatures all over the island popping up out of nowhere. They've all returned to their normal size!'

Frankie came running through the trees shouting 'AMEEEEEELIA! Where are you? I'm sorry for always being such a SNOOT. *Ameeeeelia*?! *Amelia's frieeeeends*?! *Prince Booooy*?!'

When she appeared and saw Amelia standing next to Ricky and Graham, she stopped in her tracks. 'Phew!' she smiled with relief. 'I mean, WHERE have you been?! Skiving off so that WE have to go on a wild gooseberry chase looking for you ALL night!' she harrumphed. Then added quietly. 'I'm glad you're okay though. It's boring when there's no one to compete with for badges and grades.'

Amelia grinned. The rest of the Rainbow Rangers gradually appeared, covered in twigs and mud and various bugs.

The last to make his way to the scene was Kevin, who looked very uncomfortable.

'I am SO sorry,' he said. 'Um, I didn't realise the thing buzzing around my face last night was you.'

'In a weird and twisted way, you helped us,' said Amelia kindly. 'If it wasn't for you, we wouldn't have fallen into the water and found McJiggle, and then reunited him with Gretta Grubbikins over there.'

McJiggle gave a friendly wave. 'Well isn't this grand! Has anyone had breakfast yet?'

he called over the chitter chatter.

The young creatures mumbled and shook their heads. Amelia gave her rumbling tummy a rub. She hadn't realised how hungry she was after their long night of adventuring.

'I hear there's some delicious fruits in these parts . . .' said McJiggle as he picked a handful of sugarplums from the tree. 'C'mon, there's plenty here for everyone!'

Amelia, Florence, Grimaldi and Tangine looked a little awkward. 'Um . . . are they *safe* to eat now?' said Grimaldi.

Gretta and McJiggle laughed. 'Why yes, of course!' said Gretta. 'The curse is broken!'

'The only curse these plums are responsible for now is the curse of being FAR TOO DELICIOUS!' said McJiggle, taking a bite.

And soon all of the Rainbow Rangers were picking plums from the tree and gobbling them down.

After a whole day of munching sugarplums and dancing around the Sugarplum Tree, Ricky and Graham took the Rainbow Rangers back to the campsite.

McJiggle and Gretta joined them to share stories around the campfire. Kevin sat furthest away from the fire. McJiggle told the tales of his time under the sea, while the Rainbow Rangers roasted Midnight Marshmallows and dipped them in Gretta's famous sugarplum jam.

'Ricky,' said Graham. 'We should 'ave made a *BROKE A CURSE* badge, shouldn't we?'

'Well, it's not really your everyday activity, is it?' said Ricky.

'But they broke a whole curse,' said Graham. 'That's pretty big.'

Ricky and Graham eventually decided to

present Amelia and her friends with three brand new badges that they made from bits of scrap paper and leaves:

The *BROKE A CURSE* badge, the *BE TINY AND BRAVE* badge and the *FIND A LOST LEPRECHAUN* badge.

Amelia, Florence, Grimaldi and Tangine had all of the Rainbow Rangers listening in awe as they retold their adventures of the previous night. Tangine took it upon himself to act out the whole story.

'I think we should raise a marshmallow to Nurse Bubble,' said McJiggle.

'TO NURSE BUBBLE!' the group cheered.

'But also to my new friends, Amelia, Florence, Grimaldi and Tangine. For bringing me home!'

'TO AMELIA! TO FLORENCE! TO GRIMALDI! TO TANGINE!' cheered the Rainbow Rangers.

'And to Gretta,' said Amelia.

'FOR CURSING US?!' said Florence.

'Well, what I was *going* to say was . . . to Gretta,' said Amelia. 'For a future full of happiness, love and many, many sugarplums!'

CHAPTER 19

ONE SMALL BEACON OF LIGHT

During the rest of the half-moon holiday, Amelia's sash filled up with badges. She earned her *FOOD FORAGING* badge, the *HOP UP THE MOUNTAIN* badge and, with King Jamie's help, she achieved her *BOMBASTIC BUGS* badge.

Florence was the only one to get the *FOOD THAT FARTS* badge and every Rainbow Ranger got a *BUILD A SUMMER HOUSE FOR RICKY AND GRAHAM* badge.

By the end of the week, Amelia felt like she'd learnt so much and found she hadn't thought about being homesick once. Whilst she still missed her mum and dad, she was having so much fun with her friends – and as long as she had them, she was home.

Frankie Steinburg ended up as the Rainbow Ranger Captain much to Tangine's disappointment, but Amelia didn't mind. It didn't matter how many badges she had, because she had achieved something far bigger and better. She had played a part in bringing two creatures together who had been apart for years, and finally lifting the Curse of the Sugarplum Tree.

The gang did, however, each receive a special *SEA OF SPARKLES* badge, hand-painted by McJiggle himself. Creatures of the Light who had once been cursed and now returned to their normal size cheered on

Amelia and her friends as McJiggle presented them with their new badges. Gretta even promised Tangine that she would build a shiny new restaurant on the island to remember them by.

'May I request you call it *The Tangenius Temple of Tantalizing Treats*?' asked Tangine. To which the crowd burst out laughing, and Gretta accepted his request followed by a great big hug.

'I'm going to be sad to leave this place,' said Grimaldi as the Rainbow Rangers packed their bags.

A BUZZZZZZZZZZZZZZZZZZZZZZZZZZZZ echoed through the air as King Jamie flew down to join Amelia and her friends. He and Queen Denise had visited them every day over the week and brought tiny sacks of honey especially for Squashy.

'It was such a pleasure to meet you all!'

said King Jamie.

'I'll miss your Hall of Garments,' said Tangine sadly. He still wore his frilly outfit with pride.

'DENISE,' said Florence. 'YOU'RE THE RAREST BREED OF SLUG I'VE EVA 'AD THE PLEASURE OF TALKING TO.'

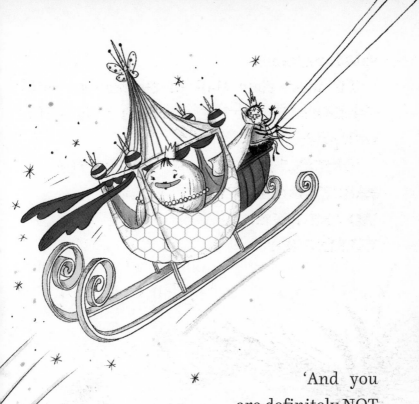

'And you
are definitely NOT
a beast,' smiled Denise.
Grimaldi bowed. 'Thank you
for helping us, King Jamie,' he said
shyly.

'You were very brave,' said the bumblicorn.
'If you were a bug, I'd have you as one of my

loyal knights!'

Grimaldi went all silly and blushed.

'Amelia Fang,' said King Jamie the Eighth. 'You and your friends will always be welcome to visit us in Buggingtonshire!'

Amelia giggled. 'We might be a little bit big,' she said. 'But of course we will!'

'Just as long as you don't try to sit on me again,' said Denise. 'Especially now!'

'What a week!' Amelia sat happily in her little stripy boat with Squashy in her lap. This time Grimaldi joined her at the opposite end, as his swirly boat was being used to transport all the jam Gretta had given to the Rainbow Rangers as a goodbye gift. The other Rainbow Rangers were all gathered together ready to sail back to the Dazzling Docks. 'I can't wait to tell Mum and Dad all about it . . . Although, they probably wouldn't believe the part where we got cursed and were the size of bugs AND then hung around in an underwater kingdom with fish tails . . . Tangine looked so funny with those tentacles, didn't he?'

But Grimaldi was curled up at the end of the boat snoring lightly. Amelia didn't blame him. It had been a very eventful half-moon holiday.

Amelia rowed and rowed across the Sea of Sparkles as the sun began to set in the sky marking the end of the half-moon holiday. She looked down at her sash full of badges and smiled. She would cherish it forever.

Amelia's arms began to grow tired. She was so close to the Dazzling Docks . . . but then as she shifted the heavy oars in her hands, they slipped into the water with a *PLOP PLOP*.

'Oh, pottering pumpkins!' she said trying to

reach them, but the oars were floating away.

Just as Amelia was about to shout for Ricky and Graham, she felt the boat begin to move forward faster and faster until it was almost flying along the water. Clinging on to the side of the boat, she peered over the edge and thought she saw a glimpse of squiggly white hair.

Amelia let the warm evening breeze brush over her until the boat sailed into the Dazzling Docks.

Grimaldi stirred and stretched. 'Oh, we're back already?!' he said looking a little embarrassed. 'Sorry. I didn't mean to fall asleep. Thanks for rowing us all the way, Amelia.'

Amelia raised her eyebrows and smiled. 'I didn't do a thing.'

As she stepped out of the boat and lifted her pumpkin backpack, she looked out to the

Sea of Sparkles, and whispered. 'Thank you, Nurse Bubble.'

On the horizon was Sugarplum Island, now teaming with creatures as it had been all those years ago. The sun had almost set, casting a deep purply-red shadow upon the island, but on its peak was one small beacon of light – the glow of the Sugarplum Tree.

After the best holiday she had ever had, Amelia felt braver than ever before. She smiled as she watched the Sugarplum Tree glow in the distance, and thought of the two creatures that would be dancing around that tree every morning and every night, for as long as they lived.

THE END

RICKY AND GRAHAM'S

RAINBOW RANGERS

BADGE HANDBOOK

I GOT THERE FIRST
BADGE

HOW TO EARN YOUR BADGE:

BE THE FIRST RAINBOW RANGER TO GET FROM ONE POINT TO ANOTHER POINT WITHOUT CHEATING.

BOMBASTIC BUGS
BADGE

HOW TO EARN YOUR BADGE:

FIND AND RECORD AT LEAST TEN TYPES OF BOMBASTIC BUG. BOMBASTIC BUGS ARE USUALLY POMPOUS IN ATTITUDE AND OFTEN CARRY A SMALL CANE.

FOOD THAT FARTS
BADGE

HOW TO EARN YOUR BADGE:

ND FIVE EDIBLE SOURCES OF FOOD THAT FARTS. ARTS MUST BE LOUD AND SUSTAINED BUT NOT NECESSARILY SMELLY

HOP UP THE MOUNTAIN
BADGE

HOW TO EARN YOUR BADGE:

MAKE YOUR WAY TO THE TOP OF THE HIGHEST MOUNTAIN ONLY BY HOPPING. ONLY ONE LEG MUST TOUCH THE GROUND AT ALL TIMES.

CREATURES WITHOUT LEGS CAN USE ONE ARM. CREATURES WITH NO ARMS OR LEGS CAN USE THEIR HEAD.

FOOD FORAGING
BADGE

HOW TO EARN YOUR BADGE:

FIND ENOUGH EDIBLE SOURCES OF FOOD FROM YOUR NATURAL SURROUNDINGS TO SUSTAIN YOU FOR ONE WEEK.

BROKE A CURSE
BADGE

HOW TO EARN YOUR BADGE:

IF YOU HAPPEN TO BECOME CURSED . . . BREAK IT.

RAINBOW RANGER CAPTAIN
BADGE

HOW TO EARN YOUR BADGE:

AWARDED TO THE RAINBOW RAINGER WHO SUCCESSFULLY EARNS THE MOST BADGES DURING THEIR CAMPING TRIP.

BUILD A SUMMER HOUSE FOR RICKY AND GRAHAM
BADGE

HOW TO EARN YOUR BADGE:

WORK AS A TEAM TO BUILD A SUMMER HOUSE BIG ENOUGH FOR TWO HANDSOME UNICORNS. HOT TUB ENCOURAGED BUT NOT ESSENTIAL*

*GRAHAM SAYS IT IS ESSENTIAL.

FIND A LOST LEPRECHAUN *BADGE*

HOW TO EARN YOUR BADGE:

FIND A LOST LEPRECHAUN AND HELP HIM TO RETURN TO HIS BELOVED AND DANCE AROUND THE SUGARPLUM TREE ONCE AGAIN.

BE TINY AND BRAVE *BADGE*

HOW TO EARN YOUR BADGE:

WORK TOGETHER WITH FELLOW RANGERS TO SUCCESSFULLY SURVIVE CHALLENGING SITUATIONS SUCH AS RAIN, FLYING AND THE S... ALL WHILST BEING THE SIZE OF A BUG.

SEA OF SPARKLES *BADGE*

HOW TO EARN YOUR BADGE:

EXPLORE AND ADAPT TO LIFE IN THE SEA OF SPARKLES.

SUPER DUPER TEAMWORK *BADGE*

HOW TO EARN YOUR BADGE:

AWARDED TO FOUR OF THE BRAVEST AND FRIENDLIEST CREATURES IN THE KINGDOM OF THE DARK AND THE LIGHT FOR WORKIN... TOGETHER AND NEVER GIVING UP HOPE.

THE RAINBOW RANGERS

PROMISE

IN THE BRIGHTEST DAY AND THE GLOOMIEST NIGHT,

WHETHER I'M A CREATURE OF DARK OR OF LIGHT,

I WILL BE PATIENT AND GRATEFUL AND KIND,

AND NEVER LEAVE A FELLOW RANGER BEGHIND.

I'LL STRIVE TO KEEP LEARNING.

I'LL TREK AND EXPLORE.

AND PROMISE TO KEEP THE RAINBOW RANGER LAW.